ADVANCE PRAISE FOR *PALE RIDER*

"The way Chuck Waters can turn a phrase and his metaphysical writing are evident in Pale Rider. *He can make this non-cowgirl want to saddle up and ride out west. If you love Westerns, don't miss this one, Mr. Waters has a gift."*

— Susan Reinhardt

Susan Reinhardt is a best-selling author and humorist and former award winning columnist for the *Asheville Citizen-Times*. Her books include *Chimes from a Cracked Southern Belle*; *Not Tonight, Honey: Wait 'til I'm a Size 6*; *Don't Sleep with a Bubba Unless Your Eggs are in Wheelchairs*; *Dishing with the Kitchen Virgin*; and *Only Hussies Wear Blue Eye Shadow*.

James pressed his right ear against the closed door of Room Six with a faint cursive "6" whitewashed into the coarse pine grain. He heard what sounded like the rustling of garments. Then heard a hoarse cough and the scrape of boot heel upon floorboards.

Not bothering to knock, James threw open the door with his left hand and drew the Colt with his right. A dissipated cowpoke, his back to James, was hitching his Levis up over his lizard-skin boots. Miss Lizzie was sprawled under a dingy gray patchwork quilt. The smell of whiskey and spent semen mingled with the fumes from a kerosene lamp set upon a nightstand near the closed window. A tattered shade of faded brown muslin was drawn down even with the ledge of the windowsill.

All the man heard was the cocking of the Colt and Miss Lizzie's startled gasp. James calmly said, "Son, I guess you never learnt rule number one in the cowboy's book of manners. Never, ever, squat on your own spurs."

PALE RIDER

CHUCK WATERS

Grateful Steps
Asheville, North Carolina

Grateful Steps Foundation
Crest Mountain
30 Ben Lippen School Road #107
Asheville, North Carolina 28806

Cover design by Arthur Wittam
Lyrics on page 2 from "Git Along Little Dogies,"
a folk song, are deemed to be in public domain.
Biblical verse page viii from King James Version
of the Bible is in public domain.

ISBN 978-1-945714-25-2 Paperback
Printed in the United States of America
at Lightning Source

FIRST EDITION

www.gratefulsteps.org

FOR MY DAD, WHO MADE
EVERYTHING POSSIBLE

AUTHOR'S NOTE

Growing up as a Baby Boomer in the 1950s and early '60s, I was about as all-American boy as you could get. Flag, country, Mom and Dad, apple pie, John Wayne, cowboys and Indians and baseball. Eddie Matthews of the Milwaukee Braves was my favorite player, and I must have spent at least a dollar in change (a hefty sum at the time) trying to find his card in the box of TOPS sealed wax packs at the neighborhood drug store. I think you got five cards for a nickel, and each came with a stiff pink slab of what was ostensibly a piece of bubble gum. Made a better bookmark than a chew.

Another big love was collecting comic books, only DC featuring the heroic exploits of Superman, Batman (my fave, he lived in a cave and liked bats), Green Lantern, Green Arrow and Wonder Woman (never quite figured out how she could deflect bullets with gold wrist bracelets, but she was HOT to a prepubescent growing boy, and that was enough).

TV also played a major role in early childhood development. "Superman" was not only featured in the color pages of a ten-cent comic book, but George Reeves was on the TV screen every week battling the bad guys who threatened the "Truth, Justice and the American Way" of Metropolis with one hand and fending off the amorous advances of ace girl reporter Lois Lane with the other.

Westerns were all over the airwaves during those halcyon days. At the peak in the late '50s and early '60s, there were dozens of western-themed shows on the air any given week. Everyone from Clayton Moore as the Lone Ranger and Jay Silverheels as Tonto to Marshal Dillon and Miss Kitty on to The Cisco Kid and Roy Rogers and Trigger. *Bonanza,* starring Canadian Lorne Green as the Patriarch of the Ponderosa, came along a bit later and was a special treat, as it was one of the first TV shows to be broadcast in "Full, Living Color."

Cowboys were a big draw at the movies, too. Saturday double-bills featuring more shoot-'em-up action than you could shake a snake at. Comic books, movie magazines, pulp paperbacks, even enticements on cereal boxes—we eagerly devoured them all. What kid didn't want a Fess Parker coonskin cap or a Chuck Connors repeater rifle? I certainly did, and my Dad—bless his heart—bought both for me as Christmas presents. I never forgot that, and that is just one of the many reasons that I have dedicated *Pale Rider* to him.

Dreams die hard, but memories live on. *Pale Rider* is in NO way intended to be an historically accurate, geographically specific work on a par with Zane Grey or Max Brand or Louis L'Amour or Larry McMurtry. Rather, I wrote it more as a "pean," an homage to the glory days when all things Wild West ruled the airwaves, filled the movie houses and spun from the presses back in the day. A profound influence on an entire generation of wanna-be gunslingers and malo hombres who longed for nothing more than to be the fastest gun west of Pecos and win the fair hand of their red-headed, schoolmarm sweethearts.

We later learned that what we saw each week on the TV or movie screen wasn't exactly true. Shootouts as shown in the opening credits from *Gunsmoke* rarely happened, and Davy Crockett's heroic demise at the Alamo did not really play out as depicted (was rather grim, actually). But it made great entertainment, and we all believed it. Back then, TV and movies and books were all we had to go on.

I had fun writing *Pale Rider* (no relation to the Clint Eastwood movie of the same name), and trust the reader will enjoy it in the spirit as intended. As for the format, I wanted it to have the look and feel of vintage pulp paperbacks, the kind you used to be able to buy for 35 cents off a metal spin rack at the corner drug store." There may be a biblical theme of redemption— if one chooses to look for it—but for the most part, just saddle up and enjoy the ride, Pilgrim.

The author is just to the left of center, proudly carrying the American flag, wearing a cap and packing not one but two pistols— locked, loaded and ready for action at a July Fourth parade, Providence Park, Charlotte, NC, late 1950s. (Photographer unknown.)

And I looked, and behold a pale horse: and his name that sat on him was Death, and Hell followed with him.

– Revelation 6:8 KJV

One

William H. "Billy" Pilgrim was sore, tired and thirsty after nearly two months of riding herd on ten thousand head of Texas longhorn on the long drive to Kansas City. He wore dusty chaps, a sweat-soaked red bandana and a faded wool shirt that was ragged with wear. His prized, hand-tooled, lizard-skin boots were caked with an inch of trail mud and cow manure. The socks inside the boots were stiff enough to stand up by themselves. He kept his ankle-length rain slicker rolled so it could double as a pillow. His meager provisions included a canteen half full of water, a few pulls of beef jerky and enough tobacco left in its pouch for a couple of roll-your-own smokes—if he rationed it out carefully.

Billy Pilgrim reined his mount and stood in the stirrups, gazing across the backs of the teeming bovines as they lumbered along, indifferent to shouts and cracking bullwhips. They were in no particular hurry to get anywhere fast, as if they were aware of the fate that awaited them in the stockyards. That was of little concern to the weary cowboy. He recalled that dour trail song the drovers would sing around the evening campfire: "Git along, li'l dogies, it's your misfortune, and none of my own." The chorus grew more raw with each pass of the whiskey bottle and was often accompanied by random yips from skulking coyotes that scouted the cattle in hopes of taking down a stray yearling.

A ridge of purple thunderheads was building along the distant horizon. Billy looked for jagged flashes of heat lightning, which could spook a herd in an instant and send it on in a mad stampede miles off the main trail. Getting the herd rounded up and settled down could take the better part of a day, and he was in no mood for any time spent backtracking. By his reckoning, they were approaching the vicinity of Destiny, and he had big plans for a night on the town.

He turned in the saddle at the sound of galloping hooves coming up fast behind him. "Hey, Billy, hold up there! Almost time to' get 'em down for the night!"

It was his trail buddy, Pete Rivers, riding hard. Billy just had to grin. Pete was covered in dust, and cactus spines bristled on the surface of his leather chaps like quills on an enraged porcupine. He looked just as tired as Billy felt.

"Whoa, Biscuit!" Pete reined his brown mare. Both man and mount breathed deeply.

"Can't be soon enough for me," Billy said. "I sure am tired of this ol' rodeo, getting an eyeful of nothing but the southern end of a northbound cow and eating jackrabbit stew and drinking boiled coffee. You think we'll make Destiny tomorrow?"

Pete Rivers removed his cowboy hat and wiped the beaded perspiration from his forehead with his yellow kerchief. "That's what the boss drover says. Lessen that rain yonder comes up and holds us back for a day or two."

Both men looked back at the southwestern sky. Little jagged flashes of white were flickering within the plum colored clouds like the tongue of some mighty primeval serpent.

Billy sighed. "Hard to say. Sometimes them storms just peter out on their own. Besides, I ain't heard no thunder yet."

Pete nodded. "Suits me fine if it just passes on by. I ain't looking to spend one more day on this damn drive than I have to."

"Amen to that, podna!" Billy reached for the canteen, which hung by a rope from his saddle horn. He uncapped it, took a swallow and passed the canteen over to Pete. He drank, swirling the water in his mouth and then spat at a horned frog as it crouched on a flat black rock in the shadow of a cactus.

Pete handed the canteen back to Billy. "Thanks. Mine's about bone dry. Need to fill it up when we get back to the chuck wagon tonight."

Both men continued on at a slow pace. A couple of the brighter stars were just beginning to emerge like pinpricks of fire in the dusking sky.

"Got any plans when we get over to Destiny?"

Billy let out a whoop. "LAWD, I mean to tell you! I'm planning to cut out early. Got some business I need to take care of, and Boss Faver said it was all right with him. First thing I'm gonna do is visit the bathhouse, take a nice hot bath to get shed of all this dirt and cow shit and then get a haircut and shave from that barber feller. Make me feel like a new man! And then, I'm gonna get a room at the Black-Eyed Susan, get a bottle and a bed. There's a little ol' gal there that I got a shine for. Hair like spun gold. Don't care if costs a month's wages. It'll be worth it, after two months in this walking cow flop. If I never see another side of beef, it'll be too soon for me."

Two

James Allbright pulled up at the Black-Eyed Susan, dismounted and walked right in, leaving the doors swinging in motion behind him. "Barkeep! Kentucky whiskey, if you've got it."

The bartender nodded and bent back to the bar. The poker action at the tables had stilled while the players sized up James. From the Colt on his hip, they knew there could be trouble if anything went down. Even the piano player had stopped his tinkling rendition of "Buffalo Gals" in mid-chorus. Chairs scraped back against the rough timber flooring. The only sound now was the empty shot glass hitting the bar.

James had drained the drink in one easy motion. He wiped his mouth with the back of his gloved hand and looked into the mirror behind the bar. Everyone was watching his reflection. He slammed down the shot glass and turned to face the room.

"WELL?" he shouted. "I'm not here to cause any trouble. Anybody know where Miss Lizzie is? I want to have a word with her."

One of the card players nodded his head upward. "Room Number Six" was all he said. James tipped his hat to the man, turned and started up the stairs. He had not passed the first step when a rough hand grabbed his shoulder. James felt himself spun around and standing face to face with a malevolent looking stranger. The man had a distinct smell of whiskey on his breath, and there was the threat of malice in his blood shot eyes.

"Hey, Mister. Just what do you want with Miss Lizzie?"

James paused, sizing up the situation. He tilted his size ten Stetson back and leaned on the worn, oaken newel post.

"Well, friend, Miss Lizzie just happens to be my wife. Now, if you have no objections, I would like to see her."

The stranger let James Allbright pass.

Three

James pressed his right ear against the closed door of Room Six. A faint cursive "6" had been whitewashed into the coarse pine grain. He heard what sounded like the rustling of garments. Then heard a hoarse cough and the scrape of boot heel upon floorboards.

Not bothering to knock, James threw open the door with his left hand and drew the Colt with his right. A dissipated cowpoke, his back to James, was hitching his Levis up over his lizard-skin boots. Miss Lizzie was sprawled under a dingy gray patchwork quilt. The smell of whiskey and spent semen mingled with the fumes from a kerosene lamp set upon a nightstand near the closed window. A tattered shade of faded brown muslin was drawn down even with the ledge of the windowsill.

All the man heard was the cocking of the Colt and Miss Lizzie's startled gasp. James calmly said, "Son, I guess you never learnt rule number one in the cowboy's book of manners. Never, ever, squat on your own spurs."

Billy Pilgrim turned to face James. The single shot from the Colt caught him right between the eyes. The report echoed like a cannonade in the dim room. A half-fastened belt buckle was still clutched in Billy's left hand. Blood had tattooed the wall behind his head with a crimson spray. There was a brief gurgle, as life ebbed from Billy's dying throat. Miss Lizzie gave out one anguished scream and fainted.

James Allbright said nothing. He turned, holstered the smoking Colt and slowly closed the bedroom door. All eyes were upon him as he descended the staircase. He motioned at the mustached man who was half-heartedly wiping a limp rag over the stained bar counter.

"Eli, I think you'll need to do some tidying up there in Room Six." James jerked his thumb upward for emphasis. "Tell Jacob over at the livery he'll need to put another pine box together. This should cover it."

James flipped a ten-dollar gold piece at the bar. It rattled against a couple of empty beer mugs until Eli smacked it flat with the palm of his hand.

"And once Miss Lizzie settles down, I'd be obliged if you would send her on home. She is in no condition to talk right now."

James Allbright adjusted the brim of his Stetson. No one made a move to stop him as walked through the swinging doors of the Black-Eyed Susan and out into the sun-split streets of Destiny.

Four

Slowly, the usual saloon hubbub recommenced, and all eyes turned to Eli Burke. He picked up the gold coin James Allbright had tossed and deposited it inside his apron pocket. Gun smoke curled under the ceiling of the staircase leading to the upstairs rooms.

"Well, Eli?" One of the poker players was still holding a draw card in his left hand. "Looks like James left you with a chore or two."

Eli Burke smacked the rag down on the bar top. "Swell. Every time that jackass comes to town with another load of cows, something like this happens. How many men has he put down now, Ace?"

"Who's counting?" Ace grinned as he flipped a black spade on top of the chips littering the green felt table. "Huh. If I had a couple of aces and eights, I'd have me a dead man's hand, just like the one poor ol' Billy never got to play."

"Well, ain't that a shame!" Eli snorted. "Clete, you better give me a hand totin' that body down the stairs. And Joe, you better run and fetch Doc Roberts, just in case James missed."

"T'ain't likely." Ace chuckled. "Not with a sure hand like he got. Don't forget, he used to be a Texas Ranger before he went sour. But, that's what a woman can do to you." He leveled a finger at Eli. "You better not let him hear you calling him a jackass. He might not take kindly to it."

Eli waved him off. "Laura, you and Betsy better go on up and see how Miss Lizzie is doing. I doubt she will be in any mood to head back to the homestead, not after what James Allbright just done."

The two whores hustled up the stairs.

Clete ambled over and waited for Eli to emerge from behind the bar. "Eli, what are we gonna do about James? He can't go on just killing every likkered-up cowhand who wants a dance with Miss Lizzie."

"Tell me something I don't know!" Eli snorted. "We ain't even got a proper jail in this town, just Woodrow Holcombe's place with a couple of iron bars set in the windows. Nearest real law we got is the territorial marshal over in Rio Brava, and no telling when he'll be passing through this way again."

Clete nodded, rubbing the scraggly grey stubble on his chin. "Well, that's a fact. But guess we ought to roust Woodrow and let him know what's going on. You reckon?"

"Yeah, yeah. But first things first. We gotta get that body out of here and the place cleaned up. And if he ain't dead, maybe he can testify against Jim. Where's Doc Roberts?"

"Ain't here yet," Clete said, "but Joe went to get him. Shouldn't be long,".

Eli sighed wearily. "Well, let's go on up see what we got."

Five

Woodrow Holcombe was pouring a dollop of gun oil onto a cleaning rag when Sarah Jane Tolliver poked her nose into the two-room adobe structure that doubled as sheriff's office and jailhouse. The one cell stood empty, and a cast-iron stove in the center of the room was cold. A dented coffee pot atop the stove balanced against the flue at a precarious angle. A chipped coffee mug sat on the desk near Woodrow's elbow. He was concentrating on rubbing down the barrel of a blue steel Smith & Wesson and did not look up until Sarah Jane spoke.

"Good morning, sheriff. I trust I am not disturbing you?"

Woodrow shifted his attention from the rag and the gun and allowed a faint smile to play. Miss Tolliver was what may be best described as a handsome woman of 30, her crimson hair always coiled in a severe bun. Her indigo eyes always sparkled as if she was constantly amused by some small, secret joke. Her figure suited her disposition, and she carried herself proudly. If she had any suitors, that fact was lost on the denizens of Destiny, although some of the biddies gossiped about a broken engagement "somewhere back East."

Woodrow put aside the gun and wiped his hands on the cleaning rag. He rose from the oaken desk chair, which creaked slightly under the heft of his two-hundred-pound frame. At six-foot-two, he could handle that weight, and he was built as solidly as an anvil. Although he was just on the hindside of 40, few men wanted to reap the whirlwind of Woodrow's bad side. Those who did usually lived to regret it. If they lived at all.

"Why, good day, Miss Sarah, always a pleasure whenever you come to call. What brings you over here all the way from the telegraph office?" Woodrow nudged the brim of his well-weathered leather trail hat with his index finger.

Sarah Jane Tolliver ventured a small jest. No telling which mood Woodrow Holcombe might be holding today.

"Oh, just my own two feet, sheriff, that's all." She paused, waiting to gauge Woodrow's reaction.

14

Woodrow Holcombe allowed himself a chuckle. "Well, I guess you are right at that. I thought maybe you had some news for me?"

She hesitated for a count and then sighed. "I do so hate to be the bearer of bad news, but it sounds like there was some trouble over at the Black-Eyed Susan. About Miss Lizzie, again."

Woodrow frowned at the prospect of having to deal with Miss Lizzie Allbright again. That usually involved a visit from her estranged husband, James, and those reckless encounters usually ended badly.

At first Sarah Jane could gain no reaction from him, but after a moment, the sheriff slammed his fist against the oak top desk, hard enough to rattle the can of gun oil he had placed there while he had been cleaning his revolver. The coffee cup rolled off the edge of the desk and broke into pieces on the wooden plank floor.

"Damnation!" Woodrow thundered, but then he immediately remembered that Miss Tolliver was standing in front of him.

"My apologies, Miss Sarah, but sounds like James has gone loco again. I thought we were done with all of that after the last time."

Sarah Jane Tolliver just dismissed the remark as if she was swatting at a pesky fly.

"No offense taken, sheriff. Living in this town, I have heard far worse, believe me."

Woodrow rose and holstered the revolver he had been cleaning. Miss Tolliver's eyes held his for a flick, and then she turned away. "Sorry to be the bearer of bad news, especially before you had your breakfast."

The sheriff made a motion as if to tip his hat, but stopped short of actually removing it. "Obliged, Miss Sarah. I guess it is best not to go off half-cocked. I would offer you a cup of coffee. But as you can see, the stove isn't fired up yet."

"Another time, then?" She closed the door softly behind as she stepped back out into the bright sunshine of the morning. A tired horse, its reins loosely tethered at the hitching post near the front steps, gave a tentative snort as Sarah Jane Tolliver passed.

Six

Doc Roberts entered Room Six carefully. Experience had taught him that whenever gun play was involved in a killing, a live round could still be fired by a trigger finger clenching in a death spasm. No such worries here. Billy Pilgrim lay flat on his back, blank eyes staring at a ceiling he had ceased to see. The bullet's entry hole in the center of his forehead was about the size of a dime, but thick dark blood had pooled onto the plank floorboards. The fetid odor of body fluid added its own cachet to the cordite and stale whiskey mingling in the closed room.

"Somebody open that blamed window, will you please!" The doctor wiped his mouth with a stained, white handkerchief and dropped his small, black satchel to the floor. The two whores, Laura and Betsy, had propped Miss Lizzie up in the room's only chair, a rickety cane-back rocker. They fanned at her pale

17

face with a yellow towel crusted with dried semen and blood. Lizzie remained motionless as the girls worked away, making comforting "shushing" noises.

The doctor gave the corpse a tentative nudge with his left foot. There was no response. A few green bottle flies had already begun a looping aerial reconnoiter of the scene. Their buzzing drone was the only other sound in the room besides the ministrations of the girls in the corner.

Doc Roberts grunted. "Well, boys, I'd say this cowboy has sown his last wild oats. Poor bastard."

He turned to the small group of men bunched in the open doorway. Some were craning their necks to get a look inside; others had already done their looking and were turning away.

"Anybody know his name? How it happened?"

There was a general negative murmur and a shuffling of feet.

"Eli? What do you know about this? Joe says you sent him over to fetch me. That right?"

The doctor looked at Joe for confirmation. Joe just nodded. One by one, Joe and the other men in the doorway drifted away, until it was just Eli and Doc Roberts alone in the room with the three women.

Doc Roberts reached into his black bag and took out a small vial capped with a glass stopper. "You gals better take Miss Lizzie over to the next room till she comes to. These smelling salts should help clear her head. I'll be in to see her directly, once I get done here."

The two whores hefted Miss Lizzie up and struggled to walk her out the door. Though not what you might call plump, the lady did fill out her dress.

"Well, Eli, let's have it. What are we looking at here?"

Eli rubbed the back of his neck as he looked down at the dead man. A few more flies had drifted in through the open window. It wasn't smelling any sweeter in the room, either, as the heat from the street shimmered up along with the insects.

"You can just about guess, Doc. Big Jim Allbright come to call."

Seven

Laura and Betsy somehow managed to maneuver Miss Lizzie into the empty room adjacent to Room Six. Doc Roberts had not even bothered to uncoil his stethoscope from his bag; just a cursory kick and a feel for a pulse on the neck had been enough of a postmortem. And, even if there had been any doubt, the dead man's unseeing and unblinking hazel eyes staring wide open at the invisible ceiling above him were testament enough.

"Well, if that don't take the whole biscuit. Jim done popped another one. And this one wasn't even carrying a gun, neither. So that makes it cold-blooded murder. Miss Lizzie is a witness to that, no two ways about it."

Doc Roberts pinched the bridge of his nose with his right thumb and forefinger. It seemed the droning of the bottle flies was growing louder, and the heat in the room was stifling. Eli still hung back in the doorway, waiting.

"Eli, better get Ace or Clete up here to help you lug this feller over to the office. We'll see if he has any identification, either on him or in his saddlebags. Most likely, he just got paid after a trail drive, and this was the first place he stopped. I guess that's what most of them boys do. Hungry for a taste."

Eli grunted and turned to yell down the hall. "Hey, Ace, quit dealing from the bottom of the deck and come up here for a minute, will ya? Lend a hand!"

The two whores had set Miss Lizzie down across the unmade bed in Room Five. Both were barely out of the teens, skinny and looking as if they could use a good meal. Laura, the brunette, was loosening the button of Lizzie's bodice while Betsy, the blonde, was working the other end, unlacing Lizzie's shoes. Both were whispering murmurs of condolence.

"There, there, honey, no man alive is worth crying over. And this one is dead as a hammer."

Laura uncapped the vial of smelling salts and passed it directly under Miss Lizzie's nose. After a moment or two, she started, jerked up, and coughed. "GOOD GODDAMN, what the HELL are you two tryin' to do, kill me? What I need now is a drink!"

Laura and Betsy just smiled at each other. Miss Lizzie was coming to.

Eight

James Allbright felt no remorse as he mounted his roan stallion and rode away from the Black-Eyed Susan and the town called Destiny. His Colt was one cartridge lighter. All he could remember was the sight of his wife sprawled under a stained patchwork quilt, and a man looking down at her as he pulled up his jeans. A sexual congress had obviously just taken place, and there was a dreamy half-smile playing across the lips of Miss Lizzie. Something deep within James Allbright had just snapped.

James thought back to his own mother, Suzannah, who had died while giving birth to a stillborn daughter. The small, white, stone marker in the Allbright family plot was now shrouded in green drape of moss and lichen, like decayed icing on a forgotten wedding cake. James had hoped to have a child of his own with Miss Lizzie. But no such issue would be forthcoming, despite his most ardent efforts to impregnate her with Allbright seed.

James's father, William, had set out for a mining expedition in the hills outside Destiny the day after Suzannah passed. He had never returned. Rumors persisted that William had either been set upon by coyotes, killed by Indians or had simply moved on west to the gold fields of California.

So, for years it had just been James and his baby sister Winnifred working the homestead, ten acres of backwoods pocked by boulders, one good stand of timber, a creek running near the cabin, a few head of lean cattle, a gaggle of chickens and a fat breed sow that constantly worried the poultry for any stray corn kernels that might fall their way. Winnie managed to coax a few beans and tomatoes and potatoes from a meager garden she kept edged with a row of sunflowers and Indian corn at the western end of the property.

It was a simple, bucolic life, at best. But that all changed on the day James returned from his monthly visit to Destiny with more than the necessary dry goods and provisions he usually carried. This time, there was a woman riding with him.

Nine

S arah Jane Tolliver walked back to the telegraph office after her visit with Sheriff Woodrow Holcombe. The man was obviously not pleased with the news she delivered, and it tickled her whenever the sheriff let his composure slip and displayed a rare flash of emotion. She couldn't blame him this time, though; the ongoing war of wills between James and Lizzie Allbright had been building for months, and it was bound to reach the boiling point soon. Everyone in Destiny knew it. She secretly hoped it would be Woodrow who would walk away unscathed.

The telegraph key had been silent while she was gone. That was good; she had not missed any dispatches. The little office had one small window, which opened onto an eastern view of the main street. A swaybacked horse was tethered haphazardly at one of the hitching posts, and a dog was gnawing a cow bone in the filtered shade of the boardwalk. Dust and horse manure steamed in the morning sun, and a mockingbird perched on the edge of the hitching post and started in with a mimic of a crow's hacking caw. She wasn't sure if the bird was attempting to torment the horse or the dog, but neither animal paid the mocker the slightest attention. The horse's tail flipped in annoyance at a stinging fly.

She sat on the stool behind the cage where the cash drawer was placed. She kept the key on a strip of rawhide, which hung from a peg underneath the counter. At night, or when the office was closed, she removed the key and placed it in the clutch handbag she always carried with her. There was never much money in the drawer, but even a couple of dollars was enough to tempt some hungover cowboy in desperate need of a taste. "The hair of the dog," they called it. She never understood the origins of that quaint and curious phrase.

Sarah Jane sighed. Sometimes, when time hung heavy and there was no business to transact, she reflected how she came to be in her particular situation. A 30-year-old unmarried woman might not be such an aberration in a big city like Boston. But out here in Destiny, she could be considered a spinster already well past her prime. And she was aware of the gossip that swirled whenever she politely declined to attend the monthly potluck social at the Church of Destiny. "She done got her heart broke back east and has been holding her love ever since," the tongues wagged.

But that was only half the story.

Ten

Winnifred Allbright walked out to the back yard to hang some wash on the line. The sun was shifting, and the shadows were coming into play.

A rider on a pale horse was approaching her, and Winnie knew the Biblical implications of that. The rider shifted his seat in the saddle. The leather creaked, and the horse nickered and pawed the brush.

Winnie held her palm above her eyes to cut the sun. She slapped at a wayward fly, and the sky was silent. It was one of those moments that come when you least expect it.

"Where is James?" the stranger asked. "We have some things to discuss and some business to finish."

Winnie picked a clothespin from the line. She eyed the stranger, not certain if there was menace in his words. He removed his hat and tipped it in her direction. Ravens were cawing.

Maybe James had some business with this man. Perhaps there was an old score to settle. Her brother had left Jawbone several days earlier on his way to Destiny, and there was no way of knowing exactly when he might return. But, she thought it best not to reveal that information to the stranger until she knew his intent.

"He is out tending to the herd and probably won't be home until dusk. I could invite you in for a cup of coffee, and perhaps you could leave him a note. I am sorry, but I did not catch your name?"

The stranger dismounted and flapped his hat at some dust on his pants. "Name is Pilgrim, miss. Aaron Pilgrim. I'd be obliged for a cup of coffee, and the horse could stand a pull of water."

"The well is right over there." She motioned with her left hand. "But be careful with the bucket, it needs mending."

Winnie turned and walked up the porch steps as the stranger lifted the bucket from the well. Usually she trusted her instincts to be right. But this time, she was dead wrong.

Eleven

Aaron Pilgrim sat down at the handmade table as Winnie tilted a battered, tin coffee pot and poured a portion into a chipped, white, china cup. Dappled daylight waltzed in a lazy swirl and mingled with sifting dust motes as the sun struggled through the opaque, yellow window glass.

"There is a little sugar in the bowl, but I am afraid the cream has gone sour." She motioned at a small butternut-colored stoneware pitcher. A fly was inching along on the underside of the rim.

"I like it black," Aaron replied and lifted the cup, sipping as he eyed Winnie. She had turned back to the brick fireplace where wood crackled and the smoke struggled upward through the listing chimney. After replacing the pot on the hearth, she straightened and smoothed the folds of her blue gingham dress over the curve of her round hips.

"Yes, ma'am, I like it black and strong." Aaron cradled the cup in his supple cowhide gloves. "So, you don't expect James back until late, then?"

Aaron Pilgrim knew James Allbright wasn't anywhere near the north acreage, nor tending to any cattle. He had seen James depart two days earlier, his shadow silhouetted against a dark ridge top as he took the left fork on the way to the town of Destiny and the saloon known as the Black-Eyed Susan.

Winnie sat down and toyed with the sugar bowl while Aaron took another sip from the cup. A few stray strands of her blond hair struggled to escape the confines of a barrette she had made from a piece of bleached cattle bone.

"Well, I hope he will be back before dark. But he took his gun with him, and sometimes that can mean trouble." Winnie immediately regretted having let that remark slip.

But Aaron just nodded quietly, saying nothing.

Twelve

Winnie Allbright sat silently, hands folded in her lap, and watched the man named Aaron Pilgrim finish the coffee and set the empty cup down on the table. The sun had slipped down behind the rimrock to the west now and cast rust colored scarecrow shadows across the floor of the cabin.

Aaron cleared his throat and pulled a silver pocket watch from a crease inside his black leather vest. As he took a reading of the time, Winnie caught a glimpse of the scar scoring the left side of his cheek. It stood out like a jagged white streak against the sunburned skin of his face.

"Gettin' on past six o'clock," he mused, talking to himself as much as to Winnie. "Does he usually stay out past dusk? Or do you just think James is a little late gettin' home this evening?"

Winnie shifted her gaze back to the window, as if the answer lay just beyond her field of vision.

"I honestly don't know, sir. He usually gets back by suppertime, but if he finds something on the fence that needs tending, sometimes he will just make camp there so he can fix it first thing the next morning."

Aaron nodded. He clicked shut the pocket watch with thumb and forefinger and returned it to the vest pocket. It was starting to darken inside the cabin, but Winnie made no move to light the oil lamp on the table. Next to the lamp was a leather-covered family Bible, open and turned to a chapter in the "Book of "Revelation." Aaron Pilgrim took notice of that.

"Been readin' the Good Book, eh, miss?"

A prairie dog chittered from a distance. A green lizard skittered across the floorboard just inside the open door. A slight puff of wind teased the threadbare muslin curtains tacked to the window frame over the dry sink.

Thirteen

"You got anything in this house to eat?" Aaron Pilgrim was eyeing a couple of canning jars stacked in an open cupboard fashioned out of an old packing crate.

Winnie followed his gaze to the shelf. "Oh, just some lima beans and apples I put up. And there might be some cornbread and bacon left in the skillet. I can't recall if I finished it this morning."

Aaron rose from his chair, hitched up his britches and ambled over to the hearth. The black, cast-iron skillet was set to the side over a bed of gray coals. A faint, dying glow burned from the center of the banked ash. The skillet was empty. All that remained was a smear of congealed bacon grease and a few golden cornbread crumbs.

"Why, there ain't enough here to keep a June bug alive. Does James usually run off and leave you to fend for yourself like this?

Don't seem right to leave a purty gal like you all by herself."

Winnie's eyes widened slightly at this. For the first time, she felt the pin-prick sensation of fear flutter within her. She found herself backing slightly away from the table and in the direction of the dry sink. A long, bone-handled kitchen knife lay atop the worn, maple cutting board.

"James doesn't usually stay gone for very long. He could be coming back over that ridge at any minute. You'll see!"

Aaron shook his head from side to side. "And after you just told me that if he ain't back by dusk, he'd just as soon stay out all night? T'ain't likely, now is it, Miss Winnie?"

He reached inside his vest pocket and withdrew a pint bottle filled with an amber liquid. He bit the cork stopper loose and spit it across the dirt floor of the cabin. A brown spider tensed in its web at the commotion, waiting.

Fourteen

Winnie's wide eyes watched Aaron Pilgrim as he took a healthy swig from the bottle. He wiped the lip of the bottle with the palm of his gloved hand and proffered the rye whiskey to Winnie. She shook her head vigorously from side to side. "NO!"

Aaron chuckled. "Why, a little taste won't hurt you none, miss. Might just help loosen up a little. Tell me, you ever been with a man before? I recollect that James had a young sister. But I didn't know she had growed up so fine."

The man took another long, sustained drink of the whiskey. His eyes had started to glow with an alcohol-fueled sheen. Winnie had seen that look before, whenever James brought a bottle home with him from one of his two-day visits to Destiny and started in on a serious drinking binge. There was little that could be done until either the bottle was empty, or

35

James had passed out from intoxication. It was impossible to reason with him once the imp had been released from the jug.

"Com'on now, li'l darlin', I won't hurt you none. Let's see what you're hidin' under that purty li'l dress."

Winnie slapped his inquisitive hand away. "Please. NO!"

Aaron Pilgrim made a sudden grab at Winnie's wrist and pulled her violently to him. "Time's a wastin', and I ain't got all night."

Winnie managed to twist away and ducked under the man's wild, off-balance lunge. Aaron's feet got tangled up with the legs of the table, and he fell backward into the fireplace. The back of his head smacked hard against the stone hearth, and he lay still, momentarily stunned. Winnie saw her chance, and dashed over to the dry sink where the kitchen knife lay on the cutting board.

Fifteen

Luke Wilkins rode up to the wooden archway bordered by pinyon and mesquite, which served as entryway to the LW Ranch. As he rounded the outbuildings, he saw his son, Jeb, hard at work laying an ax to one of the logs stacked by the woodpile. Chips flew with each grunt as Jeb brought the ax blade down hard on the log balanced on top of the broad, thick chopping stump. He was making good headway, and the timber split down the base of the pine with each stroke.

At the sight of his father, Jeb lowered the ax, lifted his straw hat and wiped his brow with a faded red bandana. Sweat ran in rivulets down his dust-creased face, and he broke into a wide toothy smile. "Ho, Jeb!" Luke hollered. "I see you got a good start on cuttin' that pile down to size, boy!"

A light breeze nudged the rusty blades of the windmill. The level of water in the well was lower than Jeb could ever remember. He lifted the ladle from the oaken bucket that sat on top of the stone well enclosure. He then offered the ladle to his father as he dismounted. A sheen of lather flecked the horse's flanks, and its breathing was labored. A lone, white puff of cumulus off toward the horizon offered no promise of rain.

"Get your business done over to Destiny?" Jeb inquired casually as his father took a small sip from the tin dipper. Luke Wilkins swished the water around in his mouth and then spit.

"Damn. More mud than water. We sure could use a good, steady two-day rain. But that ain't likely. Not this time of year, anyways."

He passed the dipper back to his son. "As to the business, well, yes and no. Got finished at the assayer's and was just heading over to the Black-Eyed Susan for a beer and a smoke when all hell broke loose. Big Jim Allbright rode into town mad as blue blazes and plugged some young'un what was laying the wood to his gal. Everybody but James himself seems to know that Miss Lizzie is a sportin' gal. Nothing can be done about it, but you try to tell that to Mister James Allbright."

Jeb just stood silently for a moment and shook his head. There were certain aspects about life that book learning had not taught him as yet, and the cruel things that men and women could inflict upon each other was one of them.

"That sure is a shame in this world, Pa."

"HUH!" Luke snorted. "That ain't the worst of it. Folks in town is getting fed up with this sort of shenanigans. Shooting a man in self-defense is one thing. But, by all accounts, this boy wasn't even carrying a gun. Talk is, they might send Woodrow Holcombe over to Jawbone to roust Jim, once and for all."

A hawk and a mockingbird were dancing an aerial ballet in the shadow of the windmill.

Sixteen

White Feather rested beside the slope of a dry wash gully. He pulled the woven blanket off the back of his Appaloosa pony and decided to make camp for the night. The moon was beginning its cantilevered climb in the western sky above the horizon, and the dog star was riding a point to the north east. Shades of crimson, orange and purple layered the landscape like the tapestry of the blanket he used as a saddle. It would be a matter of just minutes before the evening chill of the darkness would hold that sway until morning.

The Indian tossed the reins of the pony at a tall cactus. He knew his mount would not stray. It nosed at a small, yellow flower protruding from the base of the cactus and pawed the base of the succulent with an unshod hoof. Its ears perked at the forlorn wail of an unseen coyote. White Feather noted the howl, too, and after a moment, he figured the scavenger to be at least a mile away behind him. Probably caught the scent of horse droppings. White Feather always buried his own scat in the sand.

The small, leather bag White Feather carried over his shoulder held a few pulls of buffalo jerky and a small pouch of tobacco, which he had procured during his last visit to Destiny. There was enough left in the pouch for a few bowls from the clay pipe. The tequila was also running low, the worm almost visible at the bottom of the thick glass bottle.

White Feather grunted. He gathered a few scraps of dry sage branch and pinyon and built a small campfire in a makeshift circle of white stones. It took several strikes of the flint before he was able to get a spark, and he carefully coaxed a tendril of smoke to blossom into a tongue of flame. A sleek black scorpion skittered from the fire. White Feather struck silently with his knife and pinned the scorpion under the blade. With a quick wrist flick, he severed the venomous arched stinger tail, and skewered the insect with a twig and set it over the campfire. Roasted scorpion was not a delicacy, but it could be eaten.

Packing the pipe with a thumb full of shredded tobacco, White Feather held a burning sprig to the bowl and inhaled. He kept the smoke deep in his lungs for a full minute, and exhaled slowly. The skein of smoke snaked like a wraith up into the twilight.

He tilted the bottle of tequila to his mouth and took a healthy swallow. It burned his throat momentarily, but helped to soothe the harshness of the tobacco smoke. He took another drink and corked the bottle. Tomorrow, he would set off for Destiny and pick up a few provisions. Maybe stop by the Black-Eyed Susan for a hand of poker with Ace.

White Feather also had one last peyote button left in his leather bag. It was a good night to visit with the spirits. A shooting star streaked across the sky, an iridescent scar against a backdrop of velvet darkness. He swallowed the bitter button and waited quietly for the ghosts of his ancestors to come and commune with him.

Seventeen

James Allbright was tired. He debated whether to continue his ride back to Jawbone, or make camp for the night. The moon was up and illuminated the trail before him, a landscape flickering in muted shades of silver and gray. In this eerie half-light, trees became men and boulders became animals. Shadows were as elusive as smoke wisps caught by night winds and scattered like leaves in a twister.

The moon was high, but his spirits were low. Regardless of his reputation, James Allbright did not necessarily enjoy killing a man. He judged it as a necessary evil, which was part of a thankless job. More than once during his days as a Texas Ranger, he regretted having to draw the Colt and squeeze the trigger. But looking down the barrel of a loaded pistol usually left him few options. Talk was lost in the flash and thunder of gunplay.

"The quick and the dead." There could only be one winner in that deadly game of draw poker. James had been winged once or twice, but it was he who always remained standing.

His head throbbed. He decided to dismount and stretch his back for a minute, maybe roll up a smoke and take a drink from the canteen. There wasn't much water left. He always kept a pebble in the canteen so he could gage the amount of liquid it contained. The louder the pebble rattled, the less water there was inside. He tested it with a shake of his hand. The pebble knocked around like ivory dice rolling in an iron skillet.

James rolled a smoke from the tobacco sack and waited a moment before he struck a match to light it. He was listening for any unfamiliar noise on the wind. The flare of a match in darkness could be seen for a good distance. There was nothing but the lone screech of an owl hunting for tiny rodents in the desert moonlight.

He replayed the scene from Room Six of the Black-Eyed Susan in his mind. He recalled pushing through the swinging doors of the saloon, hearing all chatter and motion cease as he headed for the stairway leading to the upstairs rooms. Listening at a foolish question from some tinhorn fop. Then, the commotion behind the closed door. His hand reaching for the knob. Turning it slowly. The startled shout. The scream. And the shot . . .

Eighteen

Miss Lizzie sat up straight and shooed the two hovering whores—Laura and Betsy—off of her. "What are you trying to do to me? You could gag a buzzard with that stuff!"

Doc Roberts walked in, rubbing his hands on a handkerchief. The body of Billy Pilgrim had been carried down the stairs, out of the saloon and across the street to the rear of his office. The corpse was stretched out on a length of pine set across two sawhorses. A brightly colored blanket had been laid over it for the time being; there was nothing else that could have been done at the moment.

"Easy, now, Miss Lizzie, you've had quite a start. How are you feeling?"

"I feel just fine, thank you! But I'd feel much better if somebody would hand me a bottle. What was that vile stuff you was waving under my nose, anyway?"

The doctor chuckled. "Why, that was just some spirits of ammonia, ma'am. Helps to clean out the cobwebs. Now, do you remember what happened just before you fainted?"

Miss Lizzie sneezed and then coughed as she rubbed the back of her hand under her upturned nose. Laura had gone next door to Room Six to retrieve the whiskey bottle from the nightstand beside the ravaged bed. Betsy was trudging back up the stairs with a bucket of water and a cake of lye soap to scrub down the blood-stained floorboards. Laura popped back in just long enough to hand the bottle to the doctor, and then joined Betsy in the adjacent room to assist with the clean-up.

"Gimme a snort of that, will ya, Doc?"

He passed it over, but not before taking a liberal swallow himself. He winked. "For medicinal purposes only."

Lizzie ignored the jibe and tilted the open end of the brown bottle to her ruby red lips. Little bubbles of air rose to the top of the upended glass pint as she drained half the contents in deep draughts. Doc Roberts eyed her quizzically.

"That'll do for now, Miss Lizzie. Let me check your pulse."

Lizzie shoved the doctor's extended hand away from her left wrist. "Ain't nothin' wrong with me that a good drink and a hard man won't cure," she whooped. "I was just finishing with that cowboy when that sumbitch James Allbright busted in and started shooting. Most of these boys are so backed up, they barely get their pants down before they pop their loads. Well, at least he got his rocks off one last time. Didn't do much for me, though."

"Well, looks like your color is coming back, and you don't seem no worse for wear," Doc Roberts said. "If there's nothing else I can do for you, I best be getting back to the office to tend to the body. See if he has any papers on him. I guess we will have to cart another one up to Boot Hill, unless some kin comes to claim him. That ain't gonna set too well with Woodrow Holcombe, I reckon."

The physician turned to leave and then looked back at Miss Lizzie. "Oh! I almost forgot. James told Eli something before he left. Left him some money, so you can arrange a ride back to Jawbone?"

Lizzie Allbright's cheeks seemed slightly flushed, and she appeared to focus her gaze about two feet above Doc Roberts' domed head.

"That'll be the day."

Nineteen

James Allbright closed his eyes at the image, took a long pull from the cigarette, held the smoke till his lungs ached and slowly let it drift away on the crisp night air. It cooled off quickly once the sun set in the desert. If he was going to camp for the night, he would have to set about building a small fire and hobbling the horse so it would not roam.

He sighed. Hell, might as well just keep pressing on. Every minute on the trail would bring him closer to Jawbone, and further away from Destiny. The sordid drama he was revisiting in his head had played out twice before, and both times James had brought Lizzie back—kicking and screaming—seated in the saddle in front of him, with both of her hands tied at the wrists.

James knew that Lizzie had a wild fire blazing within her. Sooner or later, she would grow weary of the tedious family life in

Jawbone, and bolt back to Destiny and the Black-Eyed Susan for some "high living," as she liked to call it. This time, however, James Allbright was resigned. His blood boiled at the thought of Lizzie laying with another man. The undeniable fact was that she liked it. Some women regarded "coupling" as a wifely chore to be endured, but Lizzie found the act energizing, a sweet release to be pursued and savored. Her loins burned with a lust no single man could satisfy. Doc Roberts had said as much himself. "Some gals are just wired different. That's all there is to it," he reasoned.

But James Allbright loved the woman beyond all reason . . . or consolation. A black cloud had been forming in the dark recesses of his mind for quite some time, building like purple thunderheads threatening to unleash a fury of jagged lightning and crimson fire. If he couldn't have Lizzie all for himself, then no other man would, either.

Twenty

Winnie Allbright watched Aaron Pilgrim warily as he began to stir. He was flat on his back and still groggy from the smack his head had taken against the stone hearth. She stood with the kitchen knife grasped in both hands and her back to the open front door, in case she needed to make a run for it. She had taken the precaution of checking the man's pockets to make sure he was not carrying a pistol, and had bound his hands together at the wrists with a length of hemp rope she had found in the cupboard drawer. The top of her gingham dress was torn where Aaron had reached to grab her, and her ripe, full breasts were exposed through the rip in the fabric.

Aaron was slowly regaining consciousness. Attempting to sit upright, he was confused for a moment until he realized that his hands were tied. He muttered something unintelligible and attempted to roll over onto his right side.

"Stay right where you are, mister," Winnie cautioned. She extended the knife she held for emphasis. The blade of the knife had been honed to a fine, sharp edge. It had to be, in order to cut through layers of thick, tough cowhide, bone and gristle.

The man focused his eyes on Winnie's face, a tiny smirk on his mouth. "Now, now, don't be like that, Missy. All I wanted was to have a little fun. Surely there can't be no harm in that? Why don't you cut me loose and lets you and me dance a spell?"

"I ain't in no mood for no dancing, nor anything else you might have in mind, mister. All I want is for you to get back up on your horse and ride back off wherever it is you come from."

"Well, look, little lady, I can't hardly do that, now can I, all trussed up like I am? Besides, I still got that business to settle with James, as soon as he gets here."

Aaron managed to put his hands underneath his chest. Using his thigh muscles, he pushed himself to his feet. His eyes surveyed the woman and lingered on her naked breasts. His eyes still glowed with animal lust.

Dusk had enveloped the cabin. Winnie knew she needed to get a fire going in the hearth before the darkness of evening was complete. The oil lamp needed to be lit. She needed to fill the bucket from the well and get a pot of water boiling in case James returned home unexpectedly and wanted coffee. She silently prayed that he would, riding up fast over the ridge top in silhouette against the last horizontal rays of the dying purple sun.

Twenty-one

Woodrow Holcombe was leafing through a stack of WANTED posters on his desk when Eli Burke walked through the open door of the sheriff's office.

"Hey, Woody, guess you heard about the ruckus over at the Black-Eyed Susan? James Allbright walked in and shot some poor fool right between the eyes. Wanted a waltz with Miss Lizzie, looks like. And you know that don't set too well with Jim."

The bartender had a knack for addressing people by their nicknames, but he was the only one Woodrow would let get away with calling him "Woody." Sounded somehow disrespectful, and Holcombe prided himself on commanding respect. An honest man earns his respect; an untrustworthy one survives on fear.

"Yeh, Eli, I got wind of it just now. Miss Sarah over at the telegraph office just told me. Guess there ain't much happens in this small town that she don't know about. Sorry I wasn't there to stop it, but I had no idea James was back in Destiny."

Eli pulled up a slatted chair and sat across from the desk, facing the sheriff. He had turned the chair backward so his arms dangled over the backrest.

"Well, sir, far as we can figure, Jim drew on that boy just as he was hitchin' up his britches. Never had a chance, even if he had been carryin' a gun . . . which he wasn't. That's pretty cold, even for Jim. Miss Lizzie was the only other person in the room at the time. Guess I don't have to draw you a picture."

Eli felt like showing a sly smile, but the stone expression on Holcombe's face made him think better of it. "Anyway, Doc Roberts checked him out, but nothin' he could do. Me and Ace carried the body over to the Doc's office, and he is up there in Room Five at the Susan tending to Miss Lizzie right now. Funny, commotion like that usually don't bother her at all."

Woodrow said nothing, but rotated his head slowly, breaking the adhesions in his neck bones. "This dead cowboy have a name?"

"One of his amigos down at the bar said he was a drover with one of John Chisholm's outfits. Name of Billy. Billy Pilgrim." Eli paused. "At least, Jim left a ten-dollar gold piece on the bar to get him planted proper," he added.

"Well, ain't that just fine," Woodrow said. There was no emotion at all in his voice; rather, it was as if he had been debating a problem in his mind, and the solution had just presented itself.

"A man's life should be worth more than ten measly dollars, don't you think, Eli?" The sheriff arched his eyebrows at the bartender.

Eli Burke swallowed. "I reckon you're right at that, Woody. What are you aimin' to do?"

Woodrow Holcombe rose from his chair behind the desk, stood up and adjusted the leather hat on his head.

"I think it's about time Jim and I had a little talk. This killing has gone on long enough."

Eli turned to speak, but Woodrow Holcombe was already out the door and headed down the street in the direction of Sarah Jane Tolliver's telegraph office.

Twenty-two

Doc Rivers was shaking his head as he descended the staircase leading down to the ground floor and gaming tables of the Black-Eyed Susan. Miss Lizzie had the constitution of a horse, and when he left her, she was still taking shots from the bottle that Betsy had fetched from Room Six next door. The two girls were on their knees, scrubbing hard at the bloodstains that had seeped into the plank floorboards.

"You oughta take it easy on that stuff, Liz, least 'til you sure you're all right," Doc had counseled as he left the room.

Miss Lizzie just guffawed. "Don't you mind me none, Doc. Ain't been a bottle yet that I can't lick. Dunno why Jim had to up and shoot that poor boy like that. He came to see me every so often and always brought me some penny candy. Quick on the trigger, if you get my drift, but kind of sweet in his own

57

way." And with that, the memory of Billy Pilgrim pretty much vanished.

Eli was back behind the bar, wiping off mugs and shot glasses, and Ace was settling in at one of the green felt gaming tables, ready to slit the seal on a new deck of cards. A couple of chairs had been tilted forward toward the circular rim of the table to indicate those seats for the next hand were taken.

Doc Rivers motioned simultaneously to both Eli and Ace. "Let's take a little walk across the street to my office, boys. Need to talk to you a minute."

Eli and Ace exchanged glances, shrugged and followed the doctor through the swinging doors and into the dirt street. The evening was deepening. A stray mongrel snuffled along expectantly, following their footsteps.

The body of Billy Pilgrim was still stretched out on the makeshift table adjacent to the side door of the doctor's office. Flies were hovering above the striped blanket that covered him; a smear that looked like wet red moss had seeped from underneath the plank.

"Whew! He ain't smellin' any better, is he, Doc?" remarked Ace, reaching for a handkerchief from his right hip pocket. "How long you gonna leave him up there like that? Buzzards are gonna get wind of it pretty soon. Not to mention a stray dog or two here." Ace wheeled and gave the inquisitive mutt, which had been trailing them, a swift kick in the ribs with the toe of his pointed boot. The dog yelped and bolted for the safety of a nearby wagon, where it crouched underneath and watched the proceedings with hungry, yellow eyes.

"Well, by rights we ought to leave him be for a couple of days in case any kin want to come and claim the body. Maybe pack him in sawdust and ice until Jacob gets that box ready. Didn't you say he was one of Chisholm's cowhands, Eli?"

"Yep, near as we can tell. Had a pay receipt in his pants pocket. Was an 'X' next the name 'William H. Pilgrim' on the paper. Guess the boy never learned how to read or write."

"Hmmph." Ace snorted. "Well, at least he could read enough to tell an ace from a jack. He sat in for a hand or two whenever he was in town. Never had much luck, as I recall."

Eli nodded. "Spent most of his time upstairs. Think he had a thing for Miss Lizzie."

Doc Rivers slapped Eli on the back with the palm of his left hand. "And he weren't the only one, was he? Which brings me to why I asked you fellers over here. We all know this is James Allbright's coin. How many is it now, three men he has sent down? Woodrow ain't gonna put up with this no more. I know him and James were friends at one time, but this might be the final straw that tears it."

"What'll you reckon the sheriff will do?" Ace ventured. "And what do we do with this dead boy's body in the meantime?"

"As to the latter, I heard that Chisholm's drive is about a day's ride south of Destiny right now. Guess we can wait that long to see if anybody in that outfit knows if this Pilgrim feller had any kin 'round these parts," suggested the doctor.

Eli picked it up from there. "And, as to the former, last time I saw Woodrow he was headin' up the street in the direction of that telegraph gal's station. I suppose we'll all find out directly."

Twenty-three

White Feather could smell the cattle before he could see them. Ten thousand head of prime Texas longhorn left a trail of stench thick enough to cut with a Bowie knife. Not only that, but buzzards circled above the bovines in ever widening arcs, keeping mostly to the fringes and to the rear of the main herd where a stray calf or diseased bull might fall. Then, there was the cloud of dust that rose from the sand and adobe flatlands in their wake. The low, pervasive rumbling of the cattle calls. The Indian sat still on his pony's back and watched the distant spectacle.

There was no need in trying to outflank them; on his fleet pony he could easily overtake the lumbering herd. The drovers who zipped in and out like yapping dogs probably would not catch sight of a slim red man riding alone. There was no cover to speak of; the cattle train had pretty much trampled everything in its path.

White Feather surveyed the sky. The sun had already begun its slanting descent toward the painted horizon, streaked with muted shades of red, orange and brown. And sometimes purple, when the rays hit the buttes just right. A few insignificant wisps of cloud drifted across the vast blue canopy, like tufts of milk thistle borne on a wayward breeze. The effects of the peyote button he had ingested the night before at his small campfire were wearing off. He had seen visions in the fire and heard voices murmuring a strange dialect in the darkness. More than once he thought he could feel shadows moving in on him, strange apparitions that seemed to have no feet. A premonition of danger draped itself across his shoulders. Or, was it only the saddle blanket he had wrapped about him to ward off the night chill?

After a time, he nudged the pony's ribs with his heels and moved along at a slow gait. At its current pace, the cattle company would probably reach the outskirts of Destiny the next day. White Feather was determined to reach the town before they did. He was overdue for a visit to the gaming tables and a room upstairs at the Black-Eyed

Susan. And, one of his spirit visitors had whispered that Sheriff Woodrow Holcombe would be in need of his assistance.

He pulled the pony's reins to the left and pressed on silently about a mile west of the vast herd.

Twenty-four

Sarah Jane Tolliver was out back of her telegraph shack tending to her makeshift garden. She had fashioned a planter box from discarded railroad crossties and filled the bin with spadefuls of soil from the compost heap she built from a piece of chicken wire and a row of tree limbs. She added eggshells, chicken bones, coffee grounds, potato skins, orange rinds and apple peelings whenever these scarce items were available. Finding some manure to work into the odorous mix was never a problem; it was readily available, fresh from the main street of Destiny.

A few stalks of corn, some tomato vines and jalapeño and habanero pepper plants were thriving in the small beamed enclosure. She had positioned the planter facing the south and west so it would catch the midday and afternoon sun. She had bordered the little garden with a row of bluebonnets and brightly colored pansies. The solitary rosebush she had grafted from a cutting had not fared so well. The green foliage was turning brown around the edges, and the bush had not yet succeeded in producing a bud among the thorns.

She clipped a bunch of the cheery bluebonnets and carried them back inside the office. She had a vase made from one of Doc Roberts' old brown apothecary bottles, and she inserted the stems of the bluebonnet flowers into the neck of the bottle. Hardly an elegant arrangement, but it would do nicely, set on the windowsill above her telegraph key.

Sheriff Woodrow Holcombe mounted the two steps leading from the street to the door of Miss Tolliver's office. The door was slightly ajar, and he knocked lightly on the jamb to announce his presence.

"Why, do come in, sheriff, I have rather been expecting you," she said. She removed the straw hat she had been wearing while gardening and hung it on a nail next to the back door of the telegraph shack. "What may I do for you?"

Woodrow removed his dusty hat as he entered and held it between both hands. The way the sunlight struck her as she stood in silhouette against the open door reminded him of Elizabeth. He was lost in thought for a moment until Sarah Jane Tolliver prompted him. "Well, Mr. Holcombe?" There was just the hint of a smile in her voice.

The sheriff quickly regained his composure. "Beg pardon, Miss Sarah, didn't mean to intrude this way. I just wanted to thank you for bringing me that news about James Allbright. I appreciate it. Can't truthfully say it was much of a surprise, though."

Miss Tolliver turned and sat down in the swivel oak chair behind her desk. "I was afraid of that, sheriff. Wish I could deliver only good news, but we have to take what comes, don't we? Won't you sit down?" She motioned toward a ladder-back chair situated opposite the desk.

"Fine." He seated himself in the chair and set the hat he had been holding on the desktop. "I was thinking that I had best send a wire to Marshal John T. Chance over at Rio Lobo. Let him know what James has done this time, and also to let him know that I aim to ride over to Jawbone, and bring him back for holding until the next time J.T. comes through Destiny."

Sarah Jane Tolliver looked at the silent telegraph apparatus and then at the twin stacks of sent-and-received telegraphs on her desk. The piles were kept in place by a rustic railroad spike, which served as a paper weight.

"Are you planning to go after James all by yourself?"

Sheriff Woodrow Holcombe sighed. "Appears I have no choice, Miss Sarah. This killing of his has gone on long enough, and it is high time to put a stop to it. Folks are demanding action. Time to bring some law and order to this territory. There's a cattle drive coming through town in the next day or so. Things are stirred up enough as it is. Can't have the situation getting out of hand any more than it already is."

Miss Tolliver toyed with a pencil, rolling it back and forth between her fingertips. "That won't be an easy chore, will it, sheriff? I mean, considering that you and Mr. Allbright used to be friends . . . back when you two rode together with the Texas Rangers."

Woodrow Holcombe sagged inside, but his face was a mask. It still hurt, even after all this time.

"Well, now, I reckon most folks know about that, Miss Sarah. Ain't no big secret about it. But how did you happen to learn of it?"

She smiled, and took a blank sheet of telegraph paper from the stack on her desk, pen poised ready to write. "You'd be surprised what I know about you, Mr. Holcombe."

Twenty-five

Back in his office, Woodrow Holcombe reached into his front, shirt pocket and removed a thin brown cheroot. He retrieved a wooden kitchen match from a box and dragged the match across the stone paperweight he used to anchor various dispatches on the desktop. The stone was a large chunk of iron pyrite, better known in these parts as "fool's gold." Woodrow kept it around as tangible evidence of a hard lesson learned years earlier, when gold was found near the mining camp that boomed overnight into a settlement soon to become "Destiny." Woodrow winced at the recollection. James Allbright had factored into that equation, as well.

He walked over and stood looking out the window, which was framed with stout shutters. The sun was rising above the rooftops of the structures across the dirt street, and the sky was clear. Heat was already shimmering in the distance, and the smoke from his cigar felt raw and harsh in his throat.

Woodrow knew what the two-day ride to Jawbone would entail. He would have to ask Jacob at the livery to saddle up his chestnut mare, Streak, (so named because of a white blaze down her muzzle). He would lay in some jerky and an extra canteen, and maybe slip a pint of redeye into the saddlebag as well. Load the Remington rifle in the saddle sheath and carry some extra cartridges for his gun belt. Add a blanket and bedroll, and maybe the full length rain slicker. Rain was scarce of late, but it could boil up without warning. All it took was a slight shift in the wind and a lone thunderhead to trigger a sudden deluge.

He would have to find White Feather. A Mexican/Apache mix, White Feather was a keen scout and crack shot, and had helped Woodrow out more than once. After the Indian wars had quieted down, White Feather had wandered into Destiny and soon developed a taste for rye whisky and white-skinned women. He was fascinated by the piano at the Black-Eyed Susan and also proved to be a quick learner at five-card draw poker. His English was rough, but the messages that flashed from his unblinking stare were usually enough to get his point across. Although a half-breed, there must have been some other "spice in the soup" back along the line, for White Feather's eyes were the color of green jade, and threads of copper blazed within the strands of his jet black, shoulder-length hair when the sun hit it just right.

Finally, Woodrow would have to see if Luke Wilkins' boy, Jeb, might be available to watch the jail for a couple of days. Jeb worked his father's spread, the LW, and although not officially a deputy, he had helped Woodrow in the past when he needed a back-up. Jeb had not fully mastered his ciphers as yet, but he was lean, lanky and tough as a rope. He knew one end of a pistol from the other. Moreover, he was not opposed to mixing it up. Woodrow had seen Jeb flatten a drunken cowpuncher twice his size.

The sheriff pondered all of this while the Regulator clock on the wall ticked on.

Twenty-six

Luke Wilkins wasn't surprised to see Sheriff Woodrow Holcombe approaching the LW, riding in slowly just as the sun was spreading a lemon cast to the eastern sky. After all the recent commotion in Destiny, he had been rather expecting it. With the sunlight hitting him in the back, Woodrow's face was in shadow. Luke couldn't tell what expression he was carrying. Luke slung a handful of corn kernels at some chickens as they scratched in the dirt around his boots.

"Ho, Luke!" Woodrow greeted the elder Wilkins with his arm raised. Jeb was just emerging from the outhouse and was buttoning his trousers. He walked over to where his father was standing, and both watched as Holcombe reined in and dismounted Streak.

"Howdy, sheriff. What brings you out this way so early this fine morning?"

Woodrow Holcombe slapped at a fly that was noisily orbiting his Stetson. "You couldn't spare a cup of coffee for a wandering hobo, could you, Luke?"

Luke grinned at the joke. At least he now knew what kind of mood the sheriff was sporting.

"Why, I think we can manage that, can't we, son? Let's all head over to the house yonder. I think there is still one cup left in the pot on the stove."

Luke slapped Woodrow on the back, and the trio walked over to the front porch of the house. "Looks like a fine day comin' on, Pa," Jeb offered.

"Umm, might be at that. But let's see what Sheriff Holcombe here has to say about it. Fetch that coffee pot and bring an extra cup, will you, son?"

Jeb nodded and disappeared inside the kitchen. Luke motioned at the wooden, slatted rockers on the front porch, and both men sat down.

"Well, Woodrow, what's on your mind? I'm sure this ain't exactly a social call, now is it?"

Woodrow Holcombe grinned. "That's what I like about you, Luke. Not much point talking about the weather. You probably already know why I'm here."

Jeb Wilkins returned from the kitchen and handed Woodrow a white mug of oily black coffee.

"Obliged, son."

Jeb stepped down to the front stoop and sat, his back to the two men. He looked off to the east, where the sun had just about erased all of the early morning stars from the brightening canopy. He had a sense of what his father and the sheriff would be discussing.

Woodrow took a sip of the potent coffee. Luke liked it strong enough that it could almost eat through the cup.

"Guess you heard about that ruckus over in Destiny the other day? James Allbright got into a tussle with some young cowboy named Billy Pilgrim, one of John Chisholm's hands."

Luke allowed a small laugh. "Sounds like more than a tussle, Sheriff. From what I hear, James shot that Pilgrim feller stone-cold dead. Hit him right between the eyes. Never had a chance. Does that sound about right?"

Woodrow Holcombe took another drink from the mug, winced, and then slung the rest of the coffee over the porch rail. "Dang, Luke, what do you put in this stuff, axle grease?"

"HA! Me and the boy just like it strong, that's all. But I admit it does take some gettin' used to, at that."

Holcombe grunted. "Well, I ain't there yet. But you are right about one thing. James came calling at the Black-Eyed Susan and found Billy in a tryst with Miss Lizzie. If you get my drift. And, we all know how James Allbright feels about that kind of carrying on."

He waited for Luke Wilkins to reply, but there was no comment forthcoming.

"Seeing as how this is the third time James has pulled something like this, I'm afraid I have no choice but to ride over to his place in Jawbone and roust him. Folks around town want to put a stop to it. And I can't rightly say that they are wrong about that, either."

"That ain't gonna be no easy chore for you, is it, Woodrow? I mean, knowing James as you do?" Luke Wilkins wasn't looking at the sheriff now; his gaze was focused on his son's back as Jeb sat on the front porch.

Woodrow shook his head. "No, sir, it ain't. But we just can't have no more of this gunplay. Shooting a man in self-defense is one thing, but this was cold-blooded murder. Which is what brought me over here this morning, Luke. I'm fixing to head out over to Jawbone later this morning. Probably be gone for a couple of days, at least. Was hoping Jeb here could ride back in to Destiny with me. Hold it down in case there's any trouble while I'm gone. Like he's done a couple times before. Especially since I hear that cattle drive will be passing through any time now. That is, if you can spare Jeb from his chores?"

Jeb Wilkins felt two pair of eyes focused on his back as he sat on the stoop. He waited. After a pause, he heard his father speak up.

"Well, it's fine by me, but I reckon that's something you had best ask Jeb himself, sheriff. What say, son?"

Twenty-seven

L aura and Betsy had done the best they could to erase the bloodstains from the rough plank floor of Room Six. Laura rose from her knees, stretched her back and drooped a copper-colored rag into the bucket of soapy water. "Lawd, I tell you this is one chore I can do without!"

Betsy stood up beside her and wiped her hands on the apron covering the front of her purple dress. "Amen to that. All this killin' sure does get old. I will never understand the way men carry on the way they do."

Miss Lizzie had been standing in the doorway, hands on hips, watching the two girls commiserate. "Well, I will tell you ladies one thing that's for certain: most men ain't worth troubling over. And the sooner you learn that, the better off you will be."

The whores spun on their heels, startled by the woman's pronouncement. Laura rushed over and took Lizzie's arm. "Are you sure you should be up and around, ma'am? Doc Roberts said best thing you could do right now is sleep. Said you might still be suffering from shock or something." Betsy just nodded meekly in agreement.

"P'shaw!" Lizzie snorted. "Take more than a little shooting to keep this girl down. Ain't much I haven't seen in all my years. Betsy, honey, would you run on downstairs and see if Eli can spare another bottle to keep me company in my time of need? That's a good girl."

Betsy nodded. She lifted the bucket by its leather strap and left the room. The faint odor of cordite and death still permeated the walls and floor. No amount of lye soap and elbow grease would remove that anytime soon. "Guess ol' Room Number Six will be off-limits for a spell," Lizzie said under her breath.

Laura surveyed the room—the crumpled bedspread on the floor and the muslin curtain ruffling slightly from the breeze through the open window. Lizzie watched her as she walked over to the window and leaned out, catching a draught of fresh air. The midday sun cast a stray ray inside the room; it highlighted the delicate contours of Laura's face. Although barely out of her teens, lines and creases were already faintly visible under her eyes and around the corners of her downturned mouth. For just a moment, Lizzie thought she was seeing a vision of herself from ten years ago. Like a phantom photograph from an album she had long since discarded in her attic of lost dreams.

"Tell me, honey, how did you and Betsy come to find yourself in this infernal place?" Lizzie walked over and put her arm around the slight girl's shoulder. "Would you like to talk about it?"

Laura was confused by Miss Lizzie's offer of comfort. Rough as she appeared outwardly, there was evidently a soft, tender side to the older woman's personality. One that she rarely revealed.

"I-I'm not sure what you mean, ma'am." Laura snuffled. "That is, I ain't exactly sure how I came to be here myself. It just seemed to . . . happen?"

Just at that moment, Betsy returned from her trip to the bar and handed a new bottle of rye whiskey to Lizzie. "Compliments of Mr. Eli." She grinned. "Says it's on the house. For services rendered. Whatever that means!" Betsy giggled. Although Laura and Betsy were roughly the same age, it was apparent that Betsy had not quite lost all of her childhood innocence. Not yet.

"Tell you, what, ladies! Let's take this golden nectar our kind host has been so gracious to provide and adjourn to the next room. Let us leave this abattoir and allow the dearly departed to rest in peace. Come, and I will tell you a true story to ponder while we sample this fine libation."

The two whores looked at each other, eyes wide with surprise. They had never heard Miss Lizzie speak quite so glibly. And they did not understand some of the words she had employed.

"Come on, then, shall we?"

Laura and Betsy shrugged and followed Miss Lizzie out the door and into Room Number Five of the Black-Eyed Susan.

Twenty-eight

Winnie Allbright watched silently as Aaron Pilgrim tested the sharp, hemp cord which bound his wrists. "Gonna be gettin' dark pretty soon, little lady. Why don't you cut me loose, and I'll go out and gather up some firewood and get a fire going? Ain't no point in us sittin' 'round here in the dark together, is there?"

Winnie shifted the knife in her grip and took a step backward toward the open door. "I think I like you where you are just fine, mister." She tried to put a steel edge to her voice, but it just came out sounding hoarse. But the fact of the matter was that she was not feeling strong at all; an urgent need to pay a visit to the outhouse was building within her. All of the excitement had her bowels in a knot, and she knew she would have to relieve herself soon.

Aaron Pilgrim seemed to sense her discomfort, and grinned. "Nature askin' you to pay a call, miss? You know you can't just stand there and hold it in forever. Would be most unladylike, wouldn't it now?"

His coarse chatter wasn't helping the situation any. Winnie bit her lower lip and shifted her stance. "I would appreciate it if you would not use that kind of language, Mr. Pilgrim. I suspect James will likely teach you some manners when he gets back. You just wait and see."

"Ha! Not my manners I be worryin' about, missy! Me, I got all the time in the world. But you are startin' to look a mite uncomfortable, standin' there like that. Why don't you just take a little walk out back? As you can see . . ." Aaron held up his bound wrists for her. "I ain't likely to be goin' anywhere, since you got me all tied up like this."

Winnie had no choice but to risk it. It should only take a minute or two, and better to go now instead of waiting until it got pitch dark outside the cabin. She backed away slowly, holding the knife with both hands before her as she carefully stepped toward the open door.

"You just sit tight, mister. I can hear pretty good and will know if you try anything. So you just stay right where you are. I will be back directly."

Aaron made a gesture with his hands as if to tip his hat. "Anything to oblige a lady in distress, ma'am. Chivalry ain't dead. Not by a long shot."

Winnie always dreaded the short trip to the "necessary house," even in the best of circumstances. It was dark, dank and smelled of manure, moldering moss and lye. Spiders loved nesting in there, and more than once she had spied a coiled rattlesnake announcing its presence under the splintered wooden bench that served as a seat.

There was no time for investigative precautions now. She sat gingerly and felt a wave of relief pass through her. Cleaning herself as best she could with a page ripped from a mail-order catalog, Winnie exited the small structure and paused outside the door of the cabin, her ears keen to pick up any sound from within. There was nothing but silence, and the solitary HOOT from a barn owl looking for rodents in the tall grass bordering the worn path from the outhouse to the cabin.

Twenty-nine

Ace was shuffling cards absent-mindedly at the green felt table, hoping to get an early afternoon game going. The commotion upstairs had all but quieted down. The two whores were tending to Miss Lizzie, Eli was back behind the bar hooking up a new keg of brown draught beer to the tap, and Doc Roberts was over across the street trying his best to keep the flies off the body of Billy Pilgrim. There was the occasional spin of the roulette wheel, but the evening's gambling action wouldn't really get going until after the sun had set and cowpokes started to drift in for an evening of drinking and card play.

A shadow loomed outside the swinging doorway leading into the Black-Eyed Susan. Ace glanced up and caught the angular, hawk-nosed profile of White Feather as he peered inside the room. He was waiting for his eyes to adjust to the dim interior before he stepped from sunlight into shade. White Feather counted a couple of idlers bending elbows at the bar and then spotted Ace warming up a new deck. He pushed through the doors and walked over to Eli and made a measuring gesture with his thumb and index finger, indicating that he was ready for a shot of whiskey. Eli had anticipated him, and had the glass poured and ready. White Feather nodded his thanks, picked up the jigger and sidled over to Ace.

"Playing a little one-hand draw, eh amigo? No action today?"

Ace laughed, and motioned for White Feather to pull up a chair at the table.

"HA! You want action, you should have been here earlier this morning, my redbone friend. Big Jim Allbright came bustin' in, found Miss Lizzie upstairs with some poor cowpuncher and shot him dead right between the eyes. You know how James feels about that woman. Flipped a gold piece on the bar, told Eli to clean up the mess and walked right out like he had just finished eating lunch. Reckon Woodrow is gonna have to mosey on over to Jawbone and round up James this time."

White Feather grunted and flipped his old black slouch hat on the felt tabletop. "Had a feeling something like this come. Been building for a long moon. Heard it in the wind." He tossed off the shot in one swallow.

Ace nodded. "Yep. Figure things be comin' to a head this time. Ain't gonna be pretty neither, given the history between them two. So, what brings you back to town? Been awhile."

"Big cattle drive heading this way. From trail, I figure it pass Destiny tomorrow. Thought I might take room upstairs and have long sleep. Then try luck with cards you deal. No magic fingers this time, OKAY?"

Shuffling the deck with a one-handed flourish, Ace winked at the Indian. "Tell you what, let's cut for a drink. High card wins, low card pays. Savvy?"

White Feather reached over and lifted about a third of the deck from the table. He tilted the cards at Ace so he could see what was showing.

"Jack of Diamonds. Not bad. Let's see how I do."

Ace flipped over the very next card in the pile. It was the Ace of Spades.

White Feather didn't say a word. But his eyes were smiling.

Thirty

J eb Wilkins was sitting on the steps of his porch. His father and Woodrow Holcombe were standing behind him. The sheriff had asked Jeb whether he would be interested in riding back to Destiny while Woodrow rode over to Jawbone to apprehend James Allbright for the killing of Billy Pilgrim in Room Six of the Black-Eyed Susan.

The young Wilkins boy had been turning over the proposition in his mind. True, he had helped the sheriff out when he had been shorthanded a time or two, but Jeb wasn't sure he wanted a steady diet of "deputying." Visits to town usually meant trouble, and this one figured to be no exception, especially with a bunch of thirsty and trail-weary cowpunchers fixing to hit town. That would mean bar fights to break up, and random gunplay from drunken yahoos.

"You fixin' to go after James right now, sheriff? Wouldn't it be better to wait until that cattle drive has done come and moved on? Bound to be a fair passel of trouble. Usually is, whenever one of them outfits comes through."

Jeb turned and regarded the sheriff expectantly. Woodrow just shook his head.

"Nope. Best go after Jim now while I got it in mind. Longer I wait, worse it might get. He might get to thinking he got away with it again. Need to get this settled once and for all. Besides, I wouldn't think there should be too much trouble. Just a few rowdies wetting their whistles and blowing off some steam. I got a hunch White Feather will be checking in. He usually does when there is a drive coming through. He seems to sense it. Win some wampum from the tinhorns. He and Ace got a nice set-up going there. Between the two of you and Eli, ya'll should be able to handle any ruckus before it gets started."

Jeb considered this, and then looked over at his father. "What do you think, Pa?"

Luke Wilkins shrugged. "Up to you, son. I can spare you here for a couple of days, and I think the sheriff is willing to pay you his usual deputyin' fee of ten dollars. Ain't that right, Woodrow?"

Woodrow Holcombe nodded. "That's right, Jeb. Like last time. Got it all set aside for you."

Jeb thought he might be able to put that sawbuck to good use, maybe get a new hat and a couple of those paper-bound dime novels he liked from the dry-goods store.

"Well, all right then. Guess there ain't no reason not to, long as you two are all right with it. Lemme toss a few things into my saddle bag, and I'll be with you directly, sheriff."

A little whirling dust devil swirled in a momentary spiral as it kicked up a few scattered dried leaves in the yard. Then, it disappeared as quickly as it had formed.

Thirty-one

Laura and Betsy followed Miss Lizzie into Room Five of the Black-Eyed Susan, eager to hear the story she had promised them. They were unfamiliar with the meaning of some of the words she had spoken and were curious as to the revelations behind them. They had always suspected that there was more to Miss Lizzie than met the eye, that she had a history rarely broached.

Miss Lizzie had seated herself in the cane-backed rocker and motioned to the girls to sit down on the single bed in the bare room. The only other furnishings were a spindly bedside table and a stained dresser with a china basin and pitcher on top. A drab gray towel hung limply from the hinged mirror on the cabinet. For whatever reason, the mirror had been tilted upward, so its reflective surface was facing the ceiling.

Elizabeth Brevard Allbright raised the amber bottle in a toasting gesture toward the two girls. "Salutations to you both, my dear children. Now, before I begin my soliloquy, please share a taste of this divine ambrosia with me, won't you?"

The girls looked at each other curiously, and then back to Miss Lizzie. "Oh, take a damn drink, will you!" Lizzie exclaimed.

The girls nearly jumped a foot from the bed. Neither Laura nor Betsy had developed much of a taste for whiskey, considering the deleterious effect it usually had on those who imbibed it. But Miss Lizzie was proffering the bottle insistently, and Laura reached over and took it. She gave the open lip a tentative sniff, scrunched her nose in distaste and took a delicate sip. She coughed and passed the bottle over to Betsy, who did likewise before handing the pint back to Lizzie. She chuckled at the girls' obvious distaste for the rye whiskey.

"HAW!" She smacked the arm of the rocking chair with the open palm of her left hand. "Took me a little while to get a liking for it, myself. But pretty soon, you'll get to like it better than pure mountain spring water. Just takes some folks longer than others, that's all."

Both girls nodded dutifully, but it was Laura who spoke up. "Yes, Miss Lizzie. But I sure don't know why you like it so much. That nearly burnt me a new gullet."

Miss Lizzie let out a raucous guffaw. "Just you wait, girl. You'll soon develop a taste for things you never imagined. And that's just one of the things I mean to tell you. You see, I wasn't always the dissolute specimen you see sitting here before you now. Once upon a time, I was a fine thespian—actress, if you prefer. I was a featured performer at Le Chat Noir in New Orleans. That's in the French Quarter district, you might have heard of that? No? Well, *quelle domage, mes petite enfants.*"

The two whores sat wide-eyed with amazement.

"You . . . you used to be on the stage?" Betsy blurted out. "Like we seen in them picture books?"

"Then how come you wound up clear over here in a godforsaken hole like Destiny?" Laura exclaimed.

Miss Lizzie leaned back in the rocker and drained the remainder of the rye. "That is a long story indeed. Let us just say that I traded one stage for another, and that has made all the difference."

Thirty-two

Woodrow Holcombe left Jeb Wilkins at the jail and rode over to tell Sarah Jane Tolliver that he was leaving for Jawbone to apprehend James Allbright and bring him back to Destiny. He was dreading the two-day ride and, what was more, the inevitable showdown with the man whom he had once called his friend. That was before fate took a hand and shoved things sideways, when they should have been straight up and down.

He dismounted Streak and walked into the telegraph office. Miss Tolliver was making entry notes in a ledger in her fine hand. She looked up as Woodrow entered. "Well, from the looks of you, I'd say you have it in mind to go and fetch Mr. Allbright, sheriff. Is that so?"

Woodrow nodded and tipped a forefinger at the brim of his Stetson. "Yes, ma'am, you got it figured just about right. Guess I knew this day would come sooner or later, but I have been dreading it just the same. Wanted to stop by and see if there was any news from Rio Bravo before I leave." He took notice of the way Sarah Jane was regarding him, as if she found some secret mischief in his plight.

"No, sir. Nothing since that last dispatch I sent earlier. You figure Mr. Allbright will suspect that you are coming after him?"

"If he is half the man I remember him to be, I surely think he will."

The woman nodded and closed the cover of the ledger. "I understand, of course. So, who will be keeping law and order in this fine little haven during your absence? I hear there is a cattle drive that should be passing through Destiny any minute now. Some of those boys can get a little rambunctious when they have been on the trail for such a spell."

The sheriff gestured with his right thumb over his shoulder. "Got Jeb Wilkins over at the office right now. As you might remember, he has helped me out before. Between him and Eli and Ace, they should be able to handle any trouble before it gets started."

Sarah Jane Tolliver shook her head in agreement. "I surely hope that is the case, Mr. Holcombe."

"So do I, Miss Sarah. The way I figure it, I should be on my way back here just about the time that trail drive is ready to leave. Provided

I don't run into any unforeseen trouble along the way, that is."

Woodrow Holcombe was stepping to the door when Sarah Jane called him back.

"Just one thing, Sheriff. How do you think Miss Lizzie will feel about you bringing her husband back to Destiny in irons?"

Woodrow stiffened his back and turned to face the woman directly. "Well, Miss Sarah, I suspect she won't take kindly to it at all. But we will just have to cross that creek when we get to it, now won't we?"

Sarah Jane Tolliver watched as Sheriff Woodrow Holcombe mounted up, directed the horse with a right hard pull of the reins and headed east to Jawbone. She wondered silently if she would ever see him again.

Thirty-three

Winnie Allbright decided to circle the cabin once before she entered. She wanted to see if the horse Aaron Pilgrim rode in on was still tethered to the tree out back. It was, ears pricked forward as Winnie tiptoed past. She would have been relieved to find it gone and the man with it. Occasionally nibbling at a scruff of fern at the base of the tree, the horse was still waiting patiently for its pale rider.

There was still no sound from within the small rustic dwelling. Winnie paused and then chanced a peek into the rear window. Aaron Pilgrim had flattened himself against the interior wall, so he couldn't be seen through the window or from outside the door. He had managed to remove the hemp cord from his wrists by working the knot back and forth; Winnie had not been able to cinch it tightly enough. But he knew the girl still held the heavy knife in her hands. One quick jab might be all she would need to inflict a serious wound. His revolver was still tucked inside the saddlebag strapped to his horse's saddle.

Evening shadows had darkened, and the moon had not yet risen above the silent horizon. It was as if all pigment had been drained from the earth, and Winnie's sense of perspective was lost. She thought it might be wise to bide her time and remain standing outside the front door. Sooner or later, the man inside would do or say something to reveal his presence. But as the evening gathered itself around her like a cloak slung over indifferent shoulders, the chill of night was descending. Winnie had no coat, and she knew she would have to stoke up the fire in the hearth before the dying pink coals winked out like the last fading strains of a forgotten melody.

Winnie wet her lips and ventured a call. "Mr. Pilgrim? Are you all right? I am coming inside now, please stand where I can see you. I still have the knife. I don't want to hurt you, but I will if you leave me no other choice. Is that clear?"

A leaden minute passed . . . and then another. There was no response to her plaintive query. She edged quietly along until she was standing just outside the open door. Gingerly, she lifted her right foot over the threshold, and then followed with the left.

Suddenly, without warning, she felt two strong hands grab her by both ankles, pull upward and slam her down on her back. Winnie's head bounced hard against the joist, and she felt the wind escaping from her lungs. The knife flew sideways from her grip. There was no time to let out a cry.

Aaron Pilgrim loomed over her, hands no longer tied. With his right hand he slapped Winnie sharply across the cheek; it stung enough to bring tears. And with his left hand, he grabbed the front of her gingham dress, already partly torn from the previous encounter. With a rending shred, he ripped away the rest of the garment, leaving Winnie naked from the neck down. He had also resumed his singular conversation with the pint bottle of whiskey and had almost finished it off. He did so with a final flourish and flung the empty bottle in the direction of the fireplace. It shattered among the ashes laid in the stone hearth.

"Weeelll, I reckon we done put this off long enough, missy. Now, this shouldn't hurt too much. Now iffin' you don't kick up a fuss. But if you do, well, this is just a reminder as to who is in charge here."

For emphasis, the lust-fueled inebriate backhanded Winnie's other cheek with another stinging slap. Winnie felt the tell-tale taste of salty blood at the corner of her mouth.

"PLEASE! DON'T HURT ME!" Winnie sobbed, her eyes wide with terror. She had seen livestock breed and dogs and cats mate, but she still could not quite imagine that men and women did the same thing. It seemed an abomination to her, even though she had read the story of Adam and Eve after expulsion from the Garden of Eden.

Aaron Pilgrim kneeled over her and pinned her right arm down with his knee. With his right hand, he began tugging down the rest of Winnie's tattered gown; the only undergarments were a yellow cloth slip hitched around her middle. His breath was a toxic vapor of alcohol fumes, and his glassy eyes shone with malevolence. "Dunno why gals have to get gussied up in all these do-dads," he was muttering more or less to himself. "Damn waste of time!"

Winnie had tried to beat the man off with her free left hand, but her soft blows fell like butterfly wings dancing over green fields of sweet clover. She felt herself going numb—from shock and the anticipation of what was to come. When Aaron Pilgrim had her completely stripped naked, he leaned over her and winked.

"You remember askin' me what business I had with your brother? Well, don't see no harm in tellin' you now. I heard that your brother shot my only son dead last time he was in Destiny. Billy wasn't hurtin' nobody, just in town to play a few hands and sow a few oats at the Black-Eyed Susan. From what I hear, James never give Billy a chance, just plumb walked up and shot him cold. I guess you can understand now why we got a little score to settle, Jim and me? And I figure there ain't no harm in havin' a roll with his sister in the bargain, is there, Miss Winnie Allbright?"

The last thing Winnie remembered before she fainted was the sound of Aaron Pilgrim unfastening his silver belt buckle.

Thirty-four

Eli and Ace were getting set up for the evening rush at the Black-Eyed Susan. Laura and Betsy had returned from their conversation with Miss Lizzie in Room Five, where they left her reclined in the regal splendor of an alcoholic swoon. They were still buzzing over the tale of her glory days on the stage of Le Chat Noir in New Orleans. She had mentioned that some of her finer silk gowns were still tucked away in a steamer trunk somewhere and promised both girls that they could take their pick from the wardrobe one day.

"Can you imagine!" Betsy giggled. "She used to sing and dance . . . and everything!"

"Wonder if she can still remember all the words to them songs!" Laura rejoined. "Have you ever heard her sing before? I can't say as I have."

"You gals best quit that gabbin' and get painted up for the evening," Eli called. "Them cattle boys are likely to be comin' on in directly. White Feather says that drive is on the outskirts of town now."

Ace flipped a rogue high card face up from the deck he was working. "Hope them dudes is in the mood for some five-card-draw. I'm feeling lucky tonight."

"Luck come with wind. Let cards speak truth," White Feather intoned. "But sure hand help guide wind sometimes."

Ace nodded. "Amen to that, red brother! Ain't known it to fail yet. But we better take it easy, just in case one of them boys turns out to be a sore loser. Woodrow already left for Jawbone, and he got Luke Wilkins' boy, Jeb, to mind things while he's gone. He's over there right now. But we are pretty much on our own until the sheriff gets back."

Eli walked over to the table where the two men were talking. He was wiping his hands with a foam-soaked rag he had used to mop up the overflow after tapping a new keg of beer under the bar counter.

"That's a fact. For starters, them cowpokes don't take kindly to handing over their guns while they're in town. But most of 'em couldn't hit a lame jackrabbit at ten paces. Still, I recollect some whippersnapper winged Woody with a lucky shot awhile back. That poor dude never get a second chance. Doc

Roberts had to box him up when all was said and done."

The trio reflected in silence for a moment. Ace reached for a cheroot from his vest pocket, and White Feather toyed with the Bowie knife he kept tucked inside his leggings. He kept the edge honed sharp enough to split a gnat's wing. Eli gestured over to the fly-specked mirror that hung on pegs behind the bar.

"See that hole just left of that nekkid gal's teat on the painting yonder? That's where that wild shot went. Bullet is still in there. Makes for good conversation."

Before Ace or White Feather could comment on Eli's statement, the shuttered half-doors of the Black-Eyed Susan swung open. Five men, saddle-sore, tired and thirsty, paused to gauge the action in the dimly lit saloon. Then they ambled on in.

Eli sighed and slapped the rag against his pants. "Look alive, boys. Appears the cattle train just pulled in to Destiny."

Thirty-five

Woodrow Holcombe rode away from Destiny with mixed feelings, both trepidation and resolve. He was reluctant to leave the town just when the arrival of the cattle drive was imminent. On the other hand, he knew he had to apprehend James Allbright and hold him until John T. Chance could swing through and take him back to stand trial in Rio Bravo. Woodrow felt reasonably sure that Jeb Wilkins could keep things orderly in town during his absence, and Eli and Ace were available as well. Between them, they could certainly handle a couple of rowdy cowpokes fresh off the trail. Most that all of them wanted was a full bottle, a quick poke and a real bed to sleep in for a night or two.

The sun was arcing overhead. Warm rays hit the crown of his Stetson and a slight breeze played across the back of his shoulders as he rode at a leisurely pace. The fair weather figured to hold for the time it would take to reach Jawbone, and Holcombe figured he would be able to pick up signs of James' trail along the way. A scuffed rock, hoof prints in the sand, fresh horse droppings at occasional intervals. Woodrow did not feel the need to push hard but wondered quietly if his former friend would suspect that he was in pursuit. He knew the man well and trusted his instincts. What he couldn't fathom was James Allbright's fatal attraction to one Elizabeth Brevard.

He recalled the day when he and James first saw her on stage in New Orleans while they were taking a holiday from their Texas Ranger duties and spent a fortnight in Louisiana. Everything seemed different there. The humid heat that clung like Spanish moss to live oak trees, the plants and strange foliage arching out over the delta banks, the mix of French and Creole dialects and the wild music that poured from instruments with which they were unfamiliar. Both men were mesmerized by the festive spirit that seemed to emanate from every corner bistro and second-story porch. And when they first heard Elizabeth Brevard sing, it was as if the clouds parted and honey dripped. Woodrow had tried hard to banish the memories of that whirlwind escapade from his mind. While both he and James were equally enamored of "Miss Lizzie"—as she was billed on the placards outside the nightclub—it soon became obvious that she preferred the company of James Allbright to his. So much so, that during one particular evening when the three acquaintances sat down to dine at a table in one of the Quarter's finer restaurants, Miss Lizzie reached down under the table and removed a blue velvet garter from her right thigh. She proffered it to James, while Woodrow just looked on, sheepishly. Not a word needed to be said. So great was Woodrow's anguish over the rejection, that he decided to cut short his holiday in New Orleans and return to the Texas he knew would not treat him so capriciously. The affair created a permanent rift between James Allbright and himself, one which could never be mended no matter how much time passed between them.

Thirty-six

Jeb Wilkins had waved as Woodrow Holcombe dropped him off at the front steps leading up to Sarah Jane Tolliver's telegraph office. He knocked tentatively on the door jamb before poking his head inside, remembering to remove his weathered straw hat beforehand. Miss Tolliver looked up from the piece of paper she was holding in her hands and smiled at the boy.

"So, was that Sheriff Woodrow who just dropped you off? He said he might be doing that when he stopped by to visit earlier."

Jeb nodded. "Yessum. He just wanted me to check in with you before I head over to the office. Just in case any telegrams come in while he's gone. I'll be helpin' out until he gets back. Should be maybe three days at the most, unless something happens . . ." He let his voice trail off, uncertainly. The prospect of unforeseen circumstances had not really occurred to him until that very moment. Woodrow had never broached that possibility himself.

Sarah Jane noted the look of uncertainty in the boy's pale blue eyes and gave a disarming laugh. "Why, there's no need to worry about the sheriff, Jeb. There is one man who knows how to take care of himself. Trouble doesn't like to come calling at his doorstep." She paused for a moment, revisiting a fleeting memory from a distant episode. "Of course, that's not to say he doesn't bring some adversity down upon himself. Things can get unpredictable sometimes, can't they?"

She could tell from Jeb's befuddled expression that he was having trouble following her train of thought. "Well, never you mind. I expect the biggest thing you and Eli and Ace will have to worry about is a couple of boys out for a night on the town. And you have lent him a hand before, haven't you?"

Jeb nodded again, not sure what to say. "Well, yessum, once or twice. Don't know why he needs me around, though, not with them two lookin' out. And he said White Feather might be comin' round, too."

"Guess he just likes to have a big, strong fella like yourself minding the store, don't you think? I would imagine you can handle just about anything they might throw at you, Jeb."

She was teasing the boy, with no malicious intent. But the vivid red blush on the youngster's face revealed more than feigned innocence. "Reckon so, but I don't like to trouble trouble, no more than the next feller. Anyways, guess I best be headin' over to the jailhouse now. You will let me know if any more of them notes come in, won't you?"

Rising from behind her desk, Miss Tolliver gave him a reassuring look. "Now, don't you worry. I am sure things will be fine. If anything does happen, I will be sure to let you know. All right?"

Jeb Wilkins backed down the steps and replaced the hat on top of the unruly thatch of hair that sprouted from his head like wild corn shucks. "Obliged, Miss Sarah. I'll be off now."

The heat of the afternoon was building, and Sarah Jane thought she heard the distant rumble of thunder. But, more likely, it was the drumming of tens of thousands of cattle moving en masse over a vast, barren terrain of sand and bone. Soon, the herd would be mulling around the outskirts of Destiny, and Woodrow Holcombe was heading east on what she considered to be a fool's errand. She knew something of his background with James Allbright, not the least of which was the fact that both had served together as Texas Rangers. And both had courted the same woman.

James had proven the victor in that battle, and Woodrow Holcombe was duly reminded of that fact every time Elizabeth Brevard Allbright came running back to Destiny for another bender at the Black-Eyed Susan.

Sarah Jane Tolliver stifled a sigh. She knew first-hand what a woman could do to a man, and vice-versa. But this woman—this wild wanton—had debased the affections of two fine men and seemed oblivious of the emotional damage she had wrought upon them. Sarah Jane had noticed whenever Woodrow Holcombe's gaze lingered over her own fine, firm figure when he thought she was not looking. She would not allow herself to consider the possibility that the sheriff might have feelings for her. But now, Woodrow Holcombe was gone, off in pursuit of his one-time friend and fellow Ranger. And she felt a dark, perverse premonition, worrying like a mouse at the corners of her mind. Only one of the two men would survive the coming conflict.

Thirty-seven

Miss Lizzie was attending to her toilette when Eli rapped on the door of Room Six. The door was left slightly ajar, and he could see through the angular opening that the woman was stripped down to her undergarments and was washing her bare breasts with a cloth she had moistened with soapy water from a white enamel basin set upon the top of the dresser.

A clean towel hung in a fold over the top of the mirror and obscured her image from view as she lathered up with the cloth. She had added some lilac water to the bowl, and it lent a fragrant, flowery scent to the air in the little room. The opened window across from the foot of the bed let in a light breeze, which fluffed out the muslin curtain in gentle, undulating billows. Lizzie was humming a little tune to herself as she bathed and did not hear Eli's light knock.

"AHEM!" Eli announced his presence so as not to startle her and then knocked again. This time, Lizzie heard the rap and turned abruptly at the sound, arms covering her chest in a play of false modesty. Her breasts were full and round, and her erect nipples stood out like ripe raspberries against the translucence of her ivory skin.

"Land sakes, don't you know better than just to barge into a lady's boudoir without knocking?" she scolded. But it was meant in jest; Eli had seen her ample charms on numerous occasions as he tended to the comings and goings of the frequent visitors to the room.

He grinned. "Beg pardon, ma'am. Nothing I ain't seen before, you know that! But I just wanted to let you know that the cattle drive we been expectin' is here. That means you might be havin' some company soon. Quite a bit of it, I'd say. And Laura and Betsy, too. Looks like we'll all be right busy for the next couple of days."

Miss Lizzie threw the soiled washcloth down in disgust at the basin. "Eli, I kind of wish you'd let those two alone. They aren't much older than children, and some of the men get kind of rough with them. I can handle it all myself, but sometimes they get a little scared. They haven't had much of a chance to grow up proper."

Eli shook his head sideways. "Well, now, I'm sure sorry to hear that, Liz. They ain't never complained to me, and if things ever do get too rough, all they have to do is holler, and me or Ace will come runnin' to put a stop to it. And Doc Roberts is just cross the street in case there are any female complaints that need tendin' to. Besides, they are both of age, and I guess that's all that matters. Nobody forced them to be sportin' gals, now did they?"

The exasperated woman let out a raspy snort. "Goddamn you, Eli! You should know girls won't talk about that kind of thing with another man. Besides, what chance did they have for anything else in this godforsaken hell hole? They should have named this town Perdition instead of Destiny! Laura and Betsy barely know how to read and write. They have to pick that up from Miss Sarah Jane over at the telegraph house when she has time to give them a lesson or two. Sooner or later, one of 'em will have a bun in the oven, and then where will she be?"

Eli regarded Miss Lizzie with sad, red eyes and cleared his throat. "Well, ma'am, guess none of us exactly planned on windin' up here, but sometimes you just have to play the hand you're dealt. Nobody ever said life in Destiny was gonna be easy. Nor anywhere else, when you get right down to it."

"Well, that's just fine. Never figured you for a philosopher, Eli. It's a lot easier for men to just pick up and move on when things take a turn that don't suit them." She picked up the washcloth and wrung it out over the basin. "Besides, it just so happens that I am feeling a little indisposed just now."

"Well, this is a fine time to get the vapors, Liz! Reckon them two girls you are so keen on might have to pull double duty, is that it? Guess it don't matter much though, it all comes out in the wash, don't it?"

Miss Lizzie allowed herself a small laugh. "Run on now, Eli. I must finish tidying up myself, and I don't need an audience, thank you very much."

Eli grinned. "Reckon you don't at that, ma'am. I best leave you to it, then."

He turned to leave the room, and then paused to linger in the doorway. "Oh, almost forgot what else I come up here to tell you. Woodrow Holcombe done left for Jawbone to bring Jim back for shooting that cowboy you was sparking' with last time. I think his name was Billy Pilgrim? Anyway, Woody says he is gonna hold Jim until that territorial marshal from Rio Bravo comes through. Can't say Woody was too keen on going after Jim, though, given them two being ex-Rangers and all. But then, I expect Jimmy won't take too kindly to it, neither."

Miss Lizzie's face turned ashen at the news. She sat down on the edge of the bed and looked out the second-story window, the muslin gauze playing back and forth in the wind like a rippling sail.

Thirty-eight

Aaron Pilgrim stood grinning over the prostrate form of Winnifred Allbright as he shook the last few drops of semen from the glans of his tumescent penis. She had regained consciousness during the brutal encounter, but her eyes remained tightly closed, fists clinched at her sides. Aaron could not tell if the helpless girl had derived any pleasure at all from the copulation, but he most certainly had . . . and said as much.

"Well, lordy me, you shore got a tight little package on you, missy. Guess I be the first one to pluck a petal from that sweet rosebush you got between them thighs, and that's a fact. Didn't have to work very hard at it, neither. If I didn't know better, I'd say you done this a time or two yourself."

The sky outside the cabin had turned to coal. There was no sound other than the occasional nickering of Aaron's mount, still tied up near the back door of the small cabin. A fly buzzed inquisitively at the sticky dollops of ejaculate glistening like small milky beads on Winnie's pale stomach. Aaron backed away, refastened the buckle of his belt and walked over to the kitchen table. He felt around for the pint of rye on the tabletop but remembered he had drunk the last of the whiskey and had smashed the empty glass bottle to shards when he flung it into the fireplace hearth.

"HELL! A good snort would shore go good right about now, but reckon I'll just have to make do with a smoke." He pulled a small linen pouch of store tobacco from his front shirt pocket and opened the bag carefully. He removed a single leaf from a packet of golden wheat rolling papers from the little canvas sack, creased the paper between his thumb and forefinger and measured out a thin line of pungent brown flakes into the fold. The tobacco smelled like earth and wood, the leaves baked and cured from hanging in weathered gray barns over a long, slow summer of relentless heat. A simple roll between his fingertips and a moistening lick from the tip of his tongue sealed the smoke. He struck the sulfurous tip of a wooden kitchen match against the heel of his leather booth, took a deep drag, savoring the first warm rush of the nicotine as it coursed through his lungs. He exhaled slowly, aiming

116

the escaping smoke upward toward the ceiling of the cabin. He watched as it dissipated into nothingness, dismissed by a gentle gust of breeze through the open window.

Aaron Pilgrim looked down at the form of the girl he had just violated. She had still not stirred, but he could hear her slow and even breathing. "Well, now, that was sure something," he mused. "Shame you had to sleep through it. The Good Book didn't help you out much this time, did it? As I recollect, the Lord sayeth: 'Vengeance is Mine.' I figure I beat Him to it this time! Little enough payback for what your brother did to my Billy. But that's only half of what I got in mind for him when he gets back home."

The stars spun silently overhead, dancing to the immutable clockwork of the heavens.

Thirty-nine

Woodrow Holcombe was about a half-day's ride into his journey to Jawbone when he began to get that strange, prickly feeling that someone—or some *thing*—was following him. It was a tactile enough sensation to cause the hairs on the back of his neck to bristle in warning. He had learned through experience to pay heed to such premonitions. More than once, they had alerted him to some unforeseen danger, a rattler or an ambush by desperadoes in some desolate dry gulch.

He reined Streak and withdrew his boots from the stirrups. He slipped quietly down from the saddle and walked around to the right flank of the horse. He lifted its left rear leg as if to examine the hoof for a loose shoe or a pebble embedded in a nail hole. It was a cursory gesture that allowed him to glance casually behind him without drawing attention to the act. He could see no cloud of dust on the horizon behind him, and he heard no sound carried on the westerly wind at his back. The sky overhead was deep and blue, no cloud scuffing the canopy. There was the flap of a buzzard's wings as it circled lazily over some distant rotting carcass.

He crouched on his haunches and picked a couple of burrs from the horse's switching tail. He could see or hear nothing, but the ominous silence only served to confirm his fears that he was being shadowed.

"Well, hoss, appears that we got company on our trail. Best pull up and hold fast and see if somebody shows directly. Let's settle down behind this outcrop for a spell." The horse snorted as if in agreement, and man and mount moved out of view of the mesa.

Woodrow uncapped his canteen and drank three swallows' worth of water. He had to be careful with his rationing, as the nearest water hole he knew of was a day away. Best not to push the horse too hard, either. He pulled a brick of chewing tobacco from his vest pocket and carved a hunk with his jackknife, placed the brown plug between his cheek and gum and sat down to wait. The heat of the day was making him drowsy, and he nodded off in a reverie of green forest glens and mountain waterfalls cascading over boulders worn white and round as a woman's shoulders. He never heard the soft scuffling of leather feet in the sand behind him.

"Well, amigo, it is fortunate that I mean you no harm. Not good to let your guard down like that. Maybe you are getting too old for this kind of work, yes?"

Woodrow snapped to at the sound, his right hand instinctively reaching for the holstered pistol on his hip. But the holster was empty. His own gun was pointed straight at him, held steady in the firm grip of White Feather. The Indian grinned at his startled friend and handed the revolver back to him, butt-end first.

"You crazy redskin! What in blazes are YOU doing out here? I thought you was back in Destiny, minding things with Jeb and Eli while I was gone!" Woodrow was relieved that it was White Feather who had been tracking him, but he was also annoyed with himself that he had allowed his guard to lapse. In another circumstance, it might have proved fatal.

White Feather had his small, white, clay pipe going and blew a small ringed puff of smoke at Woodrow. "Saw vision in fire night before last. Things will not go well for you when you reach the man you seek in Jawbone. Figured you might need help. Si?"

Woodrow allowed himself to relax a bit. "Still watching my back, eh, friend? Well sir, I'm just glad it was you who was dogging me, and not some bushwhacker out to steal a fresh horse. But what makes you think there will be trouble ahead? James and me, we're old compadres. At least, we used to be. But I got a job to do. And he knows the code, too. Ain't that right?"

White Feather took another draw from the pipe and pointed upward as the smoke danced. "Spirit in the fire say death soon come. Spirit never lie."

He passed the pipe over to Woodrow, who regarded it as if he was being handed a coiled rattler.

Forty

Miss Lizzie raced down the stairs and grabbed Eli by the collar just as he was hitting the bottom step. "Eli, WAIT! What did you just say?" There was a pleading urgency to her voice, and it came out more as a statement than a question.

Eli spun and loosened her grip from the back of his neck, slapping her hand away. "HEY! Don't be grabbin' me from behind like that, Liz. Like to scare me witless!"

"I-I'm sorry. But you were telling me that Woodrow has gone after James? Is that right? Please, I must know!"

Eli took the woman's hand in his and walked her over past the gaming table where Ace was peeling the cover off a new deck of cards. There were a couple of players seated in chairs opposite him. A small pile of red, white and blue chips lay scattered on the green felt in the center of the table.

"You're showing a Jack high, friend. Another card?" Ace had one ready to flip from the top of the deck. The man rechecked his hand and looked at the dealer. "Reckon I will hold with what I got."

"Pat hand, eh?" Ace nodded and turned to the other player. "How about you, podna? Take a hit?"

The man folded his hands over the five cards lying face down on the felt. He glanced at his friend and then looked over at Ace. "Think I'll stand."

Ace shrugged. "Suit yourself, gents. Dealer will take one." He tossed his show card into the discard pile and added a draw card to his hand. His eyes revealed nothing, but he nonchalantly flipped a couple of blue chips into the pot. "Cost you fellas to stay in. How about it?"

Eli maneuvered Lizzie away from the game and over to the corner of the bar so they could confer privately.

"It's like I told you before, Miss Liz. James plugged that kid you was with, and you know he had no call to do that. Ain't the first time that's happened, neither. Folks is gettin' right fed up with it, and Woody means to put a stop to it. Bring some law and order to Destiny. He has Jeb Wilkins over at the jail right now to keep an eye on things, and he is set on bringing Jim back. Hold him till John T. Chance comes through next month. Sure ain't gonna be no easy chore, considering the history between them two. But I guess you would know more than I would about all of that."

Miss Lizzie's eyes welled with tears. She looked down at the worn floorboards and spoke softly. "Yes. Yes, I do know all about that, Eli. I always figured things would finally come to a head at some point. But I never expected it would be like this . . ." Her voice trailed off as she grasped the implications of the showdown looming between Woodrow Holcombe and James Allbright.

"Well, I guess that's the price you pay for playin' the field, ma'am. Ain't my place to judge. But my only question is, I wonder which of them two big ol' Rangers will be comin' back alive?"

Eli turned away from the tearful woman and began buffing a worn spot on the bar top. One of the players at the card table let fly a curse as Ace raked the small pile of chips over to his side of the line.

Forty-one

The early morning light cut across the sky like a blade of fire as James Allbright rounded the bend leading to his home. He could immediately sense that something was wrong. A few pieces of wash were still dancing in the dawn breeze, and he knew Winnie never left wash on the line overnight. She was afraid it might get snatched away in the darkness by the unseen forces that preyed on the edge of her unconscious fears. Or—more simply put—a wild scavenger or passing stranger might rip the articles of clothing down and put them to some unknown use.

He quietly dismounted and secured the reins of his tired mount to the low branches of a cottonwood tree. Stepping carefully over the uneven terrain, he approached the cabin in a low crouch, his Colt drawn and ready. He heard no sound from within, and there was no welcoming coil of smoke wafting from the stone chimney on the eastern wall. He paused, hearing a scrape of hoof around the back side of the cabin. There was an unfamiliar bay horse tied about twenty yards to the rear of the house. The horse pricked its ears as James approached it, and it let go with a questioning whinny. James cursed under his breath; he did not want to announce his presence. He stepped quickly over to silence the horse, but it was too late. Before he could turn around, he heard the metallic CLICK of a revolver hammer being cocked, and felt the cold steel shaft of a gun barrel placed right up against the small of his back.

"Drop it, friend, or you'll be dead where you stand." The raspy voice spoke without emotion, but James could detect the foul odor of stale whiskey on the breath of his assailant. "'Bout damn time you got home, Jimmy. Me and your sister been havin' a fine ol' time just waitin' on you. We got a score to settle, you and me."

James let his pistol slide from his grip and raised both hands above his head.

"That's right, easy does it. No sudden moves." Aaron Pilgrim retained the pressure of his gun barrel against James's spine. With his right boot, he kicked the discarded weapon away from where Allbright had dropped it. Then, with a simultaneous swipe

126

of his left hand, he knocked the hat clean off of James' head.

"Now, then. Turn around, easy like, and take a good look at the man who's gonna send you to hell. Just like you done to my son, Billy, you black-hearted son of a bitch."

Forty-two

Winnie Allbright had recovered herself somewhat after Aaron's assault, and she felt a warm and sticky wetness seeping from between her bruised loins. She wept quietly and gathered the shreds of her dress from the floor where Aaron had flung them, and she covered herself as best she could. She knew her life would never be the same, and she swore a silent vow then and there that she would avenge the loss of her innocence by killing the man who had stolen it from her.

Her heart leapt in her breast when she recognized James' voice speak from outside the cabin.

"I'm afraid you have the advantage of me, friend. I don't think I have ever met you before."

Then, she tensed again, as she heard Aaron's surly reply. "Well, sir, that's right funny, that is. You might not know me, but

I surely know you. 'Mister James Allbright had a gal, but couldn't keep her.' Let anyone with two bits have a poke. And that's just what my Bill was doin' when you shot him dead over at the Black-Eyed Susan the other night. Oh, yeah, I heard all about it. Word travels fast, 'round these parts. Got here quicker than you did."

His hands still held above his head, James turned slowly around until he was standing face-to-face with Aaron Pilgrim. A barely controlled rage was swelling within Aaron, and his finger was twitching against the trigger. James could tell the man was drunk, bleary-eyed and just a trifle unsteady on his feet. With one quick slap of his right hand, he figured he could knock the loaded pistol loose from Pilgrim's grip and land a solid blow to his midsection with his left. One wrong move, though, and James Allbright would be dining with the angels tonight.

He decided to stall for a moment, as he weighed his options. "Now, what makes you think I was the one who shot your son? I have been out riding fence for the last two or three days. My sister, Winnie, will tell you as much. Just ask her."

Aaron Pilgrim laughed. "HELL! Me an' that little lady already had a nice chat, Jimmy. And a bit more than that, too. I done gave her a lesson in the ways of the world. And I'd say she's a quick learner."

James Allbright felt a surge of anger rise within him. He narrowed his eyes to slits, and with one deft motion brought the edges of his hands sharply down against both sides of Aaron Pilgrim's neck, striking so quickly that the startled man did not have a chance to react. He gasped in pain as the blow shook him. His trigger finger involuntarily flexed, squeezing off a stray shot that tore into James' left foot. Aaron lurched backward at the recoil, and the pistol fell from his grip. James felt his legs buckle and he collapsed on one knee. Blood from his injured foot spurted from the toe of his boot.

Winnie had been watching the drama unfold through the cabin window, and with both men down, she saw her chance. Her dress in rags about her waist, she ran from the back door and dashed over to where James was kneeling. He was struggling painfully to rise and stand. Aaron was flat on his back, gasping to regain his breath, hands clutched around his bruised windpipe. Winnie reached down and grabbed the closest of the two revolvers that had been discarded during the altercation. She felt the eyes of her brother watching her back as she took the gun and walked over to where her assailant lay helpless. She held the pistol steady with both hands, leveled the barrel directly at Aaron Pilgrim's groin and pulled the hammer back. The last thing she remembered hearing before she squeezed the trigger was an anguished plea. "Winnie! NOOOO!"

Forty-three

Aaron Pilgrim lay dead, his lips pulled back in a death grimace and a look of terror frozen in his blank eyes. A stain of dark red blood was slowly spreading from his ruined crotch, and the only sound was a ticking of hot metal as the pistol cooled in Winnie's hands.

James Allbright was struggling to stand and pushed with both hands against the ground. He felt a stab of pain course through his injured left foot every time his heart pumped. He hobbled over to where Winnie stood over the man she had just shot, pistol still tightly gripped with both hands. Her face was a blank mask. Her finger tightened against the trigger as she contemplated firing another round into the corpse. She heard her brother coming up behind her. She felt him reach around her and remove the still-smoking weapon from her hands.

"He's dead, honey. He can't hurt you anymore. No need to waste another bullet on him."

Winnie turned and threw her arms around her brother's neck, sobbing in choking gasps. "He . . . he said he was going to kill you because you shot his son, Billy! And he said he was going to take his vengeance out on me first. He . . . he . . ." Winnie could not finish the sentence, so raw was her shame.

James stood beside her and put his left arm around her waist. "It's over now, baby. I only wish I had got here sooner, then maybe none of this would have happened. But we got to take care of our own business. Let's get you back inside the cabin and put a clean dress on you, and then we'll see about patching up my foot. Way it feels now, it is so swollen we might have to cut the boot off to get to it."

Winnie snuffled and finally turned away from the body of Aaron Pilgrim. The image of the death agony etched in his face would haunt her dreams for days and weeks to come. It would flash in and out of her subconscious mind like a stray ray of sunlight intermittently emerging and then disappearing behind a bank of thunderheads. James put as much of his weight on Winnie as he thought she could bear, and brother and sister slowly moved along to the rear door of the cabin. Aaron Pilgrim's mount pricked its ears forward, inquisitively.

"Was it true what he said, James? About you killing his son over at the Black-Eyed Susan the other night?" Winnie helped her brother slide onto one of the kitchen chairs. He noted the torn shreds of Winnie's dress on the floor, and the shards of glass from the broken whiskey bottle littering the stone hearth of the fireplace. He wished there was one last swallow left in the glass; he could have used it right then. But he had to make do with a ladle of well water from the bucket in the dry sink. He took a long drink from the dipper and then offered it to her. She took three small sips. Brother and sister regarded each other silently, still absorbing the events that had just transpired outside their little house. The scent of death hung in the air, and the heat of the day was beginning to take hold.

Winnie repeated her question, hoping that his answer would somehow help her make sense of the carnage. "Well?"

James was concentrating on his wounded foot and gingerly tested the boot. He could feel the warm blood pooling inside it. He would have to get the boot off and bandage the foot; he wasn't sure if the spent bullet passed completely through the foot, or if it was still lodged in the bone.

"Lord, that hurts. Feels like a sledgehammer come down on it. Might have to cut the boot clean off. But, yeah, I did shoot a man the other night. Didn't know it was this Pilgrim feller's son at the time. But I had a good reason, never you mind about that. I reckon we can expect some company directly, so we oughta get things cleaned up as best we can. Okay, sis?"

Winnie looked away from her brother and down at the floor. Tears welled in her sorrowful blue eyes. "It . . . it was about Lizzie again, wasn't it, Jimmy?"

Forty-four

Miss Lizzie sat and gazed quietly out the window of her upstairs room at the Black-Eyed Susan. She was still struggling to comprehend the import of the message Eli had just delivered to her: Woodrow Holcombe had left Destiny in pursuit of James Allbright and meant to bring him back to face justice. Whenever and wherever that might be. Twice before, she had fled from the confines of the Allbright domicile, and twice before she had been retrieved by her iron-willed husband. The first time, she had lasted a month; the second time, just a week. She chafed under the drudgery of playing wife to James and stepmother to Winnie. She quickly learned she was not suited to life as a hard-scrabble frontier woman. She had once shone in the stage footlights of Le Chat Noir in the French Quarter. She had debated the wisdom of choosing James over Woodrow as her suitor.

But it was too late to mend that particular fence now. Her only recourse had been to jump it like an unbroken wild mare in season.

Well, now things would be coming to an irrevocable head. She mulled the possible outcomes in her mind. If Woodrow was successful in apprehending James and bringing him back to answer a charge of cold-blooded murder, then the situation would resolve itself. James would be out of her life forever. But James was not the kind of man to be taken lightly. His temper was legendary, and Lizzie knew that the secret he and Woodrow shared had eroded what had once been a keen friendship and replaced it with a simmering hatred. A mutual respect of the other's abilities was still grudgingly evident in their behavior. But Lizzie had seldom heard James speak anything at all of Woodrow since they had parted company that fateful day back in New Orleans.

On the other hand, suppose James got the jump on Woodrow and was waiting for him in Jawbone? Surely, James would instinctively know that the sheriff would be coming after him. There might be a showdown. Gunplay. It was quite possible that one man—or even both—could wind up dead. Which man would she mourn more? And that would leave Winnie an orphaned girl of sixteen. What would become of her? Against her best intent, Lizzie had grown rather fond of the girl, and at times felt more like a birth mother than a stepparent. In fact, folks occasionally commented on more than a passing resemblance between the two women. It was just another of those annoying vexations that Lizzie had tried to sweep from her mind.

Lizzie reasoned that she was facing the most important crossroads of her turbulent life. Impulse and spontaneity had brought her to where she was now; an uncertain future was all she could foresee. No tears had fallen as yet, but she found herself sitting with a balled-up, stained, white linen handkerchief clenched in her right hand. She rose from the rumpled bed and walked over to the bedside table. Opening the single drawer, she withdrew a sheet of paper from a small, stationery box inside and dipped a quill pen in an alabaster inkwell that was on top of the table. She scribbled a few brief lines, capped the inkwell and stepped over to the open door of her room.

"Laura? Betsy? Are you there?"

It was Betsy who responded. "Yes, ma'am, I'm still here. Laura is gettin' ready to go visit with some of them cowboys in the saloon. She'll be back up here with one of them directly, I expect."

Lizzie managed a wry smile. "I expect she will at that. Listen, can you do me a favor, honey? I have a list of some things I would like from Doc Roberts, if he has them. Would you be an angel and run over and fetch them for me?"

Betsy looked puzzled by the request but just shrugged her shoulders and nodded. She glanced at the note before she put it in the front pocket of her red satin dress. She did not recognize any of the words that were written on the small folded piece of parchment.

"Of course, Miss Lizzie. Are you feelin' all right? You got kind of a funny look in your eyes. But, don't you worry none. I'll be back as quick as I can."

The girl turned and ran out the door. Lizzie watched her leave, and then softly closed the door behind her.

Forty-five

James Allbright sat on the front step of the cabin with his injured foot propped up on a pillow and the shreds of Winnie's ripped dress wrapped around it. He had to cut the boot from the top down through the sides to the sole to loosen it and carefully pull it off. The stray bullet had nearly severed the big toe from the foot, and blood had caked the sock he had been wearing. He had gingerly removed the sock and flung it away from him and poured a shot of whiskey on the wound. A splinter of bone protruded from the top of his foot, and he still felt it throb with every pulse.

Winnie had changed into her only other dress, the blue one she usually saved for Sundays and special occasions, which were few in Jawbone. She stood in the doorway of the cabin and looked down as her brother examined his wound. He winced as the sock came off and cursed silently under his breath.

"Just my damn luck for that shot to hit me in the toe like that. God damn that Aaron Pilgrim and the horse he rode in on."

Hearing the name of Aaron Pilgrim snapped Winnie from her moody reverie. She was still in a state of semi-shock, not only from the rape and from the confrontation between Aaron and James, but also from the fact that she just murdered a man. That man was lying dead in the backyard, and the other was wounded. She placed a small hand on her brother's left shoulder and cried. "Oh, Jimmy, what are we going to do now? I shot that awful man. If the sheriff comes for you, like you say he probably will, what will we say? And what will we do with the body?" Her voice had started softly, as if she was asking herself a question, but ended in a plaintive wail.

James placed his hand over Winnie's and patted it firmly. "Now, now, sis, never you mind. If you hadn't shot that bastard, I would have, especially after what he did to you. And if that was his son, Billy, who I killed back in Destiny, then I am glad I did that, too. Aaron Pilgrim was going to kill both of us, no question about that. We'll just say I shot him in self-defense, and we'll be fine, as long as you back me up on that. Okay, honey?"

He turned to face his sister. She stood with her eyes closed, tears scoring dust rivulets down her cheeks. "So, how are you feeling now? Know that must have been a hard wringer he put you through. It ain't supposed to be like that at all. Especially if it was your first time and all. I sure am sorry it had to happen like that. It can be a very beautiful thing."

Winnie snuffled and pulled her hand away from James's shoulder. "It was a first, and I hope it will be the last time, too. I didn't like anything about it.

"Try not to think about it, Win. That man can't hurt you anymore. But we got to figure what to do with what's left of Aaron Pilgrim. Don't know if he had any kin who will come looking for him, but sure as I'm sitting here, I do know that Mister Woodrow Holcombe will be looking for me. Probably been on my trail since yesterday. That gives me a day's head start, but if I know the man like I think I do, we can expect him to show by sundown."

He paused and cast an upward look as the sun reached its midday tipping point in the brooding western sky. Then he completed his thought. "Which ain't that far off. We had best get busy, sis."

Forty-six

Jeb Wilkins walked back up the main street from Sarah Jane Tolliver's telegraph shack to the Black-Eyed Susan. He stopped to gaze through the dirty glass front window of Orville Smoot's dry goods store. On one of the display tables set in front the window were a couple of new dime novels that Jeb wanted to buy with part of the ten dollars Woodrow Holcombe had promised him. *Guns at Peyote Pass* by Lassiter Millwood, and *The Durango Kid* by Buck Jones. Jeb had trouble deciphering some of the bigger words, but he liked to look at the accompanying illustrations. His father could help him make sense of some of the more difficult passages.

He ambled in and nodded to Orville, who was unpacking a crate of canned goods on an oilcloth covered table in the center of the store. "Howdy, Jeb! Ain't seen you in a spell. How's Luke?"

"Just fine, Mr. Smoot. We been busy over at the ranch, and Woodrow asked me to come in and help mind things while he went off to fetch James Allbright and bring him back from Jawbone. Sounds like he means to make it stick this time, too."

Orville, a slim man with a small mustache and wiry hands, wiped his bald pate with a red kerchief. "Yep, that was some nasty business over to the Susan. Heard James drew on that cowboy while his pants were still down around his ankles. Of course, he wasn't carrying a gun, no ways."

Jeb nodded and walked over to the table where the books were on display. He picked up *The Durango Kid* and leafed through it, smiling at the lurid picture of the Kid, blazing away with Cold Peacemakers in each hand. "These just come in, did they, Orv?"

Smoot smiled. "Yes sir, came in week before last, and they went pretty quick, too. Only got a couple copies of each one left. You want I should save one for you? I know how much you like them."

"Sure would! I'll be back to settle up after I'm done with all this deputyin' chore. The sheriff said he should be back in a couple days. I'll probably want a sack of that penny candy and a block of chewin' 'bacca for Pa, too."

"I'll have them ready for you. Now don't you worry none." Jeb reached over to shake the storekeeper's hand.

"You expectin' much trouble, with Woodrow gone and them cattle boys fixin' to hit town?"

Jeb shook his head. "I surely hope not, Mr. Smoot. That's why the sheriff asked me to lend him a hand, just in case there is. But I don't expect none."

"Well, good luck to you, son. Holler if there's anything else I can do for you."

Jeb left the dry goods store in a pleasant frame of mind, looking forward to the time when he would be able to sit down at the kitchen table back home and start in on the two little books. He took the writings to be the gospel truth, and his father did not dissuade him from that notion, even though Luke Wilkins knew that most of those dime novels were pure hogwash.

He strode back up toward the Black-Eyed Susan and noticed a couple of dusty cowboys brush through the swinging saloon doors, removing their hats as they did so. *Looks like the drive done hit Destiny,* he thought to himself.

He followed the men inside. Eli looked up from the bar where he was pouring a couple of pints of warm beer for the saddle men. Ace was holding forth at the card table and looked up at Jeb.

"There you are, podna! Glad to see you're still with us, especially since we're one man short. White Feather had one of his peyote dreams and left to catch up with Woodrow. Said he might be needing some help bringing James in. Thought there might be trouble."

Jeb removed his hat and sat down at the table. Ace was seated by himself, sizing up the boys drinking beer over at the bar. They were engaged in an animated conversation between themselves and were paying the card sharp no mind.

"Surely hope it don't come to that." Jeb sighed. "Was hopin' things would be nice and peaceful this time. Anything been happening?"

Ace shook his head negatively. "Pretty quiet so far, but things might start picking up soon." He motioned with a deck of cards at the men over at the bar with Eli.

Jeb ran his left hand through his blond thatch of hair and exhaled. "Well, them boys will be thirsty, and I reckon they will have a few before they be wantin' anything else." He cast an eye in the direction of the staircase leading to the numbered rooms upstairs. "How are them gals?"

Ace laughed. "Reckon they be getting themselves all prettied up. Could be in for a long night." He practiced cutting the deck of cards deftly with one hand.

As if on cue, a door slammed from above and Betsy came bounding down the stairs, holding the note that Lizzie had given her to take over to Doc Roberts. She raced over to Eli, and blurted: "Miss Lizzie must be feelin' poorly. She give me this note to take over to Doc, but I don't know what it means!"

Eli put down the wet rag he had been using to wipe spilled beer from the bar top. "Best let me have a look at that, Betsy." He squinted at the cursive script written in Lizzie's distinctive hand. It read: Laudanum and Iodine.

"Huh," he wondered aloud as Betsy waited anxiously. "Now, why do you suppose she wants them things for?"

Forty-seven

Woodrow Holcombe and White Feather rode side by side up the gentle rocky slope leading to the draw about a mile east of the Allbright homestead. The sun was descending in the low sky and a bright shimmer of Venus was already dimly visible perpendicular to the crescent moon. Both men reined their mounts, and White Feather pointed at a low, black swirl lazily circling a point in the distance. "Looks like trouble following in the wind. Death has come this way."

The sheriff spit a stream of black tobacco juice off to the side of his horse's front foot. "Reckon James be waiting on us to show. He ain't one to be caught by surprise. Most likely, he's sitting on his front stoop right now with a shotgun across his lap. He always could sense trouble coming from a mile off."

"So can I," the Indian said. "It waits while we wait. I see . . ."

Before White Feather could finish his thought, a gunshot echoed across the expanse of space and shattered the relative calm of the afternoon. Both men looked off in the direction of the report, and Woodrow instinctively reached for the Smith & Wesson on his hip. White Feather tilted his head curiously. The echo of the shot slowly dissipated in the light wind like the last ripple a pebble makes when tossed into a body of still water, rings gently undulating away from the source of the disturbance. They waited for the sound of a second shot, but none was forthcoming.

"Let's split up. You circle around and come up from behind, and I'll ride straight on in. If he's by himself, shouldn't be too much trouble to take him. But that shot might mean that somebody else is there," Woodrow said. "James lives alone there with his wife and sister, and we both know Miss Lizzie is in Destiny right now."

White Feather grunted. "Best go and find out." He nudged his pony gently with his heels, turned away from his companion and rode in a southeasterly direction. Woodrow watched until he disappeared from view, and then urged his own mount forward.

Forty-eight

James Allbright could hear Woodrow Holcombe coming. A clack of hoof on rock, startled fowl rising from sagebrush. He sat with his injured right foot propped on a pillow on the porch railing and leaned back in his chair, waiting. He had removed his Colt from the holster and laid it across his lap, and then he placed his hat over his gun hand, forefinger curled around the trigger grip.

Woodrow Holcombe approached him slowly, both hands raised above his head. "Howdy, Jim. Lotta frogs from tadpoles since we last saw each other."

"That's a fact, Woody. Like to say it's good to see you, but I reckon I know why you're here. You could save us both a heap of trouble if you'd just say you were passing through and ride on." James shifted his grip slightly on the gun in his lap and softly cocked the hammer back with this right thumb.

"Wish it could be that easy, but you know I can't do that, Jim. We been friends too long for that, and you know I have to bring you in for what you done back there in Destiny. Shot down Billy Pilgrim at the Black-Eyed Susan in cold blood. He was hardly more than a kid. Them other two men you killed . . . you could claim self-defense on those because they were armed. But this boy was just standing there with his pants around his ankles. Can't let that one slide, Jim. Townsfolk had enough of this free-range killing. They want justice. Got to take you in and hold you till John T. Chance from Rio Bravo comes through next fortnight. Being a Texas Ranger once yourself, surely you know that."

Both men eyed each other, unblinking. Woodrow sat on his horse, both hands still held high, looking down, and James, looking up, a grin forming at the corner of his mouth. A lone crow cawed overhead, and Woodrow's mount nickered softly at the sound. The air was still as an empty green bottle.

"Well, sheriff, what would you do if you came to town and caught some bastard pokin' your wife? Just let it slide? Oh, that's right, you don't have a wife, do you?"

Woodrow felt his cheeks color at the insult, but let it pass. "No call for that kind

151

of talk, Jim. I know we both have feelings for Elizabeth, but that was a long time ago. No point dwelling on that now, is there?"

"Maybe not. But that don't change the fact that you're still sweet on her, ain't that so? And from what I hear tell, you might have even taken a turn with her yourself every now and then whenever she gets to feeling frisky and runs back off to the Susan. Ain't that right, podna?"

Woodrow lowered both hands, grabbed the saddle horn with his left and drew his pistol with his right. James flipped the hat sideways off his lap, showing his own revolver pointing straight at Woodrow's head. Both men fired their weapons simultaneously in a split-second crescendo of smoke and flame. Woodrow was struck in the temple, knocked clean off his horse by the force of the blast, dead before he hit the ground. He landed flat on his back, his face a crimson mask and his brains oozing out into the sand beneath his head. James caught Woodrow's round flush in the chest, his heart and lungs splattered into a bloody pulp. He fell backward, gun flying from his right hand, and collapsed in a motionless heap onto the porch planking. His legs jerked convulsively for a couple of seconds, and then he lay as still as the eternal silence that washed over the bodies of the two dead men.

White Feather had snuck up unseen behind James from inside the cabin during the confrontation. Holding Winnie firmly pinned against his side, he had covered her mouth with his left hand to prevent her from crying out an alarm. But he had arrived a moment too late to intervene. He stood, watching helplessly as the bloody tableaux played out before him. He loosened his grip on Winnie, and the girl raced over to the spot where her dead brother lay. She knelt, softly stroking the curls of her brother's dark hair and weeping silently to herself. White Feather walked over to check on Woodrow but knew at a glance that nothing could be done for him. He looked down at the body of his dead friend and gently closed the lids over the sightless eyes. "The spirits are with you now, White Brother."

He turned back to Winnie and placed a calming hand on her shoulder. "Come, little one. There is nothing left for you here. It is time for you to meet your destiny. Your destiny has been waiting for you a long time now."

Epilogue

White Feather made Winnie realize that
with the passing of her brother, James, life
in Jawbone held nothing for her anymore.
She salvaged a few precious belongings,
most notably the family Bible and some of
the clothes Lizzie kept locked in a trunk and
James's prized Texas Rangers badge. The
few remaining heads of livestock were turned
loose, where they would either be assimilated
with other herds, revert to a feral nature, or
simply succumb to predators. White Feather
recovered Woodrow's sheriff's badge, his
Smith & Wesson revolver and the small
notebook he kept in his saddle bag. Rather
than dig three separate graves for Woodrow
Holcombe, James Allbright and Aaron Pilgrim,
the two survivors placed the bodies inside the
cabin and set it ablaze. They watched in silence
as the flames licked through the rustic timbers
until the fragile structure collapsed in upon

itself. White Feather took the three mounts in tow behind his lead pony, and Winnie chose to set herself behind him rather than ride one of the other horses by herself. Still numb and unable to comprehend the tragic events of the past twenty-four hours, she rode in silence, speaking only to ask for water or to dismount briefly to rest occasionally along the trail leading back to Destiny.

Elizabeth Brevard Allbright had succumbed to a lethal combination of alcohol, laudanum and iodine, and Doc Roberts was never able to satisfactorily determine whether the overdose had been accidental or deliberate. He was able to learn, however, that she was two months pregnant. Jeb Wilkins was asked to stay on in Destiny as temporary sheriff until a replacement for Woodrow Holcombe could be found. His father, Luke, hired a vagrant Chinaman named Caine to help him with the farm chores. Jeb began studying his ciphers with Sarah Jane Tolliver, who mourned Woodrow Holcombe's passing deeply. She began giving reading lessons to the young man, so he would be able to more fully appreciate the dime novels he so enjoyed. She took up pen and paper herself and began to concoct little stories of her own for future publication. Winnie let the two whores, Laura and Betsy, take their pick from the dresses she had salvaged from Miss Lizzie's trunk, and the girls began sitting in on Sarah Jane's informal teaching sessions as well. After a few months, White Feather and Winnie Allbright departed Destiny for a solitary desert sojourn to the land of his ancestors . . . and were never seen again.

ACKNOWLEDGMENTS

To Micki Cabaniss Eustler, for never giving up; Cathy Mitchell, Pulitzer Prize-winning copy editor for making the book better; and Arthur Whittam, for his "ornery gunslinger" cover photo.

ABOUT THE AUTHOR

Chuck Waters is a freelance writer currently living in Beaufort, North Carolina.

His articles and stories have appeared in various newspapers and magazines including *The Raleigh Times*, the *News & Observer*, the *Asheville Citizen-Times*, the *Carteret County News-Times*, the (Waynesville) *Mountaineer, Lumina News, Wrightsville Beach Magazine, Smoky Mountain News, This Week Magazine*, the *Spectator* and the *Independent Weekly*. He has won North Carolina Press Association awards for feature photography and graphic design. *Pale Rider* is his first novel.

Waters is currently at work on *The Devil Serves Lemonade*, his take on the hard-boiled, pulp fiction genre.

There may be more.